The
Bastard
Pleasure

The
Bastard
Pleasure

Seán McGrady

DZANC BOOKS

DZANC BOOKS

1334 Woodbourne Street
Westland, MI 48186
www.dzancbooks.org

The characters and events in this book are fictitious. Any similarity to real persons, living or dead, is coincidental and not intended by the author.

THE BASTARD PLEASURE

Published 2013 by Dzanc Books

ISBN: 978-1-938103-55-1
First edition: July 2013

This project is supported in part by awards from the National Endowment for the Arts and Michigan Council for Arts and Cultural Affairs.

Printed in the United States of America

10   9   8   7   6   5   4   3   2   1

For my wife

Cecília

&

my children

Maria, Joanna, Joseph,
Nina, Michael
& Simon

Also dedicated to the eternal friendships in time,
apprehended in what was common and eventually
what was essential,
and who were *the boys in the entry*:

Friends,
Kevin Byrne,
Noel Stewart,
Ronnie McFarland
Des McAleer,
Terence Byrne.
& my brother,
Danny McGrady

All of them an endless source of inspiration and joy

The Perspective

This is a true story—only the facts have been changed.
From the film
The Seven Percent Solution

The facts are fictions. There are no facts. Certainly not like those we cling to. Worthless particulars. Nor are there particular judgements of fact. So where do we think we find ourselves with facts and the accumulation of facts? In the logical judgement, S is not P? In, if S is P, T is Q or S is P or T is Q? I doubt it. In the judgement of the senses? In abstraction? In inference? Nothing there to support the fact, but we are always content to live with half truths.

So, if not in the place of facts, as there is no such place (only the illusion of a place), where and how do we find ourselves? Ultimately in knowing the whole and not the parts. But a crucial first step in knowing that something is true is in the separation of the true idea from the illusory image.

And if the idea is justice, there is no better justice than doing justice to an idea. Justice then is what I am after. The justice that composes the soul, untouched by a mischievous consciousness. Beware the consciousness that says it is clear, beware the idea that deludes in endless duplication.

Opposition is all around so it will require immense courage, courage as a whole human act. The true idea however will introduce the comforting conatus which itself leads to the abandonment of the idea. This then, let me say, may become as simple as slipping on a satin glove.

If however, you have never been rapt in a cruel fantasy, maybe you should adopt or adapt the philosophy of *as if.* Fictions are decisive.

Fiction Friday, November 17th 1972, and the great Ulster dialectic, known as The Troubles, was in full flow. Flowing like a fully formed masochistic fantasy. The ritual cruelty was unmistakable.

Another fine fish day. I was floating in bad form to work in an Ulster downpour. At about six p.m. I arrived in the tight slum streets of the Belfast Markets in the south of the city, where uniformly unsteady British Army boys presented themselves to confront a threat, surrounding the immense Eliza Street bakery complex where the risk resided. Here they wanted to break the new Republican resolve.

The new resolve, an almost anonymous force, was soon within the body of the place, frantically exploring its dimensions, unseen in and among the night shift workers, some of whom recognised the traces. It knows not yet what exactly it is, but it proceeds. It will depend for its self knowledge on flashes of illumination as it goes.

Military orders were issued in exaggerated shouts. After the shouting there was the siege and the shooting. Inside and out, the sophisticated and savage capacities of hunters and hyenas were at work. Which, in the realm of consistency, of organisation, was to be the most powerful? What order of consistency would emerge triumphant, the sluggish and tired old order or the accelerating but chaotic new?

Work was suspended. Deafening machinery slowed to a silence leading to the composition of pertinent questions.

What shite is this? The shite that can get you killed. Why do they bring it in here? They know it's their bread and butter. The men within wanted out.

Inside, at his station in the belt room, old McGraw, of dwindling capacities and fading fortunes, no longer situating himself so much as being situated, displaced and on the edge, sectioned in his own society, slowing and on the slide, awkwardly angled to see aright, raw McGraw, in a final fling to be known, wanted, more than anything, to know me. He told me, amidst the turmoil and insecurity, that I would be safe with him.

On issuing the magic word *safe* out of the carefully crafted ritual he himself was enslaved to, trying to resurrect his old powers, he edged me towards the old, familiar intersection, having in his feeble mind a reconstruction of his early, more dynamic rhythms of life that featured him as a central figure. Struggling to find my own form, my own centre of activity and its dimensions, I took his word *safe*, subordinated myself to it, and went in his safe direction, neither subject entirely to him or myself.

The
Bastard
Pleasure

1.

My wee bird 'n diamond. That's me. That's what the mother called me out of her powerful imagination. Her, in her own relation and bound to it. A bird and a diamond. I had to be a conjurer. Two separate images in my wee head to be transformed from psychical nonsense into meaningful, agreeable signs. For that I would need an imagination like hers, and not to step far beyond it. And a capacity to express it just as she did. In tears on occasion. And a hearer to attend. Luckily, it was the prodigious period in my life, an imagination was suddenly at hand, and the mother's primitive language was perfectly adequate to address the attentive imaginative listener.

A wee bird 'n diamond. A singing thing and a shining thing. A living thing in flight and a dead motionless thing. Is a diamond lifeless? Is not every thing alive? Even the artificial, in the right arrangement. It meant I was an alive precious one. A pure moving thing. An innocent thing like an unformed animal. Uncontaminated. A thing to be loved for we can only truly love the uncontaminated individual. But there is no such thing in reality.

My wee bird 'n diamond. An idea given to preserve me in the world, so it was magical. But the mother's effort in her own relation was weak, she was not herself given many words of comfort, her contamination was great, thoughts never quickened and her body is now at a standstill after a slow, slow death. An article of non-being. Nothing for the hands to touch, an idea of dubious quality. A lively enough memory which will die as surely as my body will. Or, should I take notice of the notion that there remains something of the mind that is eternal?

The imaginative force that is the memory lives and breathes the universal. There's no living without it. At what point can I slip comfortably back into the past? Me with my half-sized hand gently nestled in the mother's, walking back together from the fever hospital. I survived the lung disease to breathe normally again, to smile again and to say hello. Sunny, dry. Too bright for anything but squinting. Over-warm in a tweedy, belted-up overcoat. All wrapped up to preserve me. Lots of life in me still, but not the contradictory still life. I lived for movement. They all said I couldn't keep still. That's Seamus, they'd say. That was me feeling healthy. Feeling like a force to be something or just to be. But the mother is now perfectly decomposed. Her warm stubby fat hand for holding has withered away. The primacy of recollection permeates.

That was then. Now, I wake up sampling the sensitivity of my right nipple. In my dream state it is Princess Urraca doing the sampling. A medieval beauty, a perfectly adjusted composition of mind with correspondingly perfect dimensions of body summoned up by spirited notions, a congregation of imaginings of the non-Humean kind. Who is in charge? Rather, what charges and discharges? Both criminal and honourable. Ethical and ontological.

Now I have to abandon those fanciful hieroglyphs. The day that it is requires a swift and steady momentum, to keep pace with the important guest, who you'll only know is there by the speed of his entry. Slipping in at the appropriate pace is his forte. Encountering him at a lesser speed will have you on the defensive playing all the forced moves. He'll slip by like a queen developing on the open diagonal, having already mucked you up with his rampaging horses and slinking bishops.

He comes to me soon enough, making tracks all the way from those Belfast markets. He says he has to be out of there for good. *It's a place of pure badness, always was, always will be.* That's something of the mother's tongue, which is becoming more and more a characteristic of his speech and a defining feature of the shape of his body in motion. The mother's motion matched her words. His attire, however, speaks of his intention to strike out with a new individuality. In his fashion I can see he won't be detained there in the dump much longer. He no longer wears the uniform, breaching the habit of the best of slum men, denying at last their solidarity and dedication to Fenian hostility. Seduced by a decent brogue with a moderate heel, he kicked off with zeal the orange Chelsea marching boots that had seen the blood of many an alien arse on them. The ones that stood on the neck of a floored turncoat before the end arrived with the application of a butcher's knife set. He bid a not so fond adieu to his native togs, the black donkey jacket with leather trim, white T-shirt and loose denims on the legs that were worn short above the Chelsea boots. He found an excellent second-hand Harris Tweed sports jacket in a rust colour on the rails of a dealer in Smithfield Market that went well with a pair of blue corduroy breeks. A checked countryman's shirt finished off the look that he described quite wrongly as aristocratic. The lining had a large red stain under the inside pocket that he said was ink from a leaking pen.

On this bleak day his arrival is as promised with a strong endeavour to kill or have me at his mercy. That would have a man on edge. He has, you might say, the cliffs of Moher at his disposal. He'd show you the view and the next thing you know he'd have you hanging there by your fingernails. I don't want to be the recipient of a dummy move with the regret that always accompanies a foolish form of anticipation. I'll have to kill him first or make him listen. I'm worried that he would defy all attempts to remove him. The easiest solution is for him to premeditate his own death. Surely he would have the decency, the grace to sacrifice himself.

He comes from a fair distance, though he knows several shortcuts through a maze of back streets and entries. He has to. It's now customary. He always says it takes no time at all, and reminds me immediately that we are the closest of relations, not through blood or situation but language. The language that defines our immediate predicament.

He brings with him all his possessions to prove it. Everything. Like he's moving in. A powerful amount of weight to bear, even though he has the body to bear it. At the very moment of his arrival out spills his goods. All in perfect order he says. Looks like a heap to me. He thinks I envy the contents and the harmony, but I don't. The harmony of a heap is not at all obvious, whereas harmony should be immediately apparent. If anything, it is a mess, and a mess I detest. I envy his name, that's all, but he doesn't know that. His name is Alan. I want his neutral name and his prejudiced ear. There were other neutral names but nothing like Alan appealed so much to my ear. I call him Alan the Listener, for that form of attention is his declared interest.

Like a church usher I guide him though the main door. Unhurried, with the merest of touches. An irritating lightness with the tips of the soft, satin fingers that makes him shiver like he's been catered for by the numinous. I avoid looking directly into his eyes. I escort him, head down, into a sphere of holy comfort, though church is the last place he wants to be. *Why does this place resemble a tabernacle? I don't need a Lord and saviour*, he repeats frequently. He claims he is himself an intercessor. *An intersector*, he would say. Elevated to the status of an inventor of words and worlds, placed in an alignment. Extended on a particular plane. That's the danger. There he'd have you suffering like a wee half-wit hallion. He has the cunning of a phony madman.

His need is plain, his plan, is to feed unsavoury ideas to any mind set on destruction. To quicken the process. He's a veteran of such conflicts. This is all part of his battlefield. Usually he appears uninvited, not even a short period of grace is given, but this time I have taken the initiative and issued an invitation. He'll eventually say I have summoned him. I aim to show him the scar, to run my finger down the red raised skin and remind him that he is the cause of it. Better still, place his finger on it and let him feel its raised contours. Unless he actually feels it he will have no true idea of it.

Listen to Seamus McGladdery's story, he would shout around the place, like a crazy evangelist of the church of the holy lobotomy, but no one would listen. They all thought he was mad. *They are mad*, says he, *if they call me mad and don't themselves listen.* So, I propose that he listens to me. We settled ourselves over a plate of high density champ, charged with plentiful amounts of scallions. Down on our chairs and up with our sleeves.

I do expect something from you, I say. *Not the passive presence or the slow response.*

What exactly? Be precise, he replies.

An acceleration of the cerebral. At the very least. Expressing your new individuality.

And what if I don't participate in the way you desire?

The usual Irish correction. I'll crack your head against the pavement.

My intention is to attention.

Stand at ease! I tell him. *I don't want any awkward formality.*

Yet that sounds like a command.

So he sits at ease with the champ and eases into conversation, every now and then crunching a savoury scallion and wincing. He tells me that he doesn't sleep because grave ideas do not allow it. He is required to think actively at all times. He dreams of being passive, just for the rest. I am hoping that the scallions will assist in dulling the excesses of his active mind.

You know how it is with a troubled mind? he says.

I do know it very well. How it is. How is it for you? And I know he knows that I know.

You cannot know without knowing that you know, he often says, but wasn't it I who inserted that idea into his head?

There is always pressure to think wisely, in a sense to leap out of time into eternity, or a mode of it, to think to some purpose, to get it together as much as possible before the set time runs out. The eternal now as it were.

The eternal now, as it were! he says. *Now as it were! A nice way to put it. But who mentioned time?*

It's the essence of the mind to strive to think without obstacles, to think adequately, a Godly sort of thinking. The link with time is obvious.

To expedite matters, he says, *I encourage you to reveal something about yourself just to me. That would help me enormously, because in you I see myself. If I could be someone else it would be you. More you than me in fact. If I gave up being me maybe you could be you.* He says this at close quarters. I don't say a word, I am enjoying a mouthful of creamy mashed potato free from a single scallion, with my mind at the same time occupied in thought by his latest comment. Is he trying to mean, if I gave up being me, maybe I could be you?

My enjoyment with the mash is apparent to him, as is my puzzlement. *Enjoy! Enjoy!* he commands. The form annoys me. Among many other activities I cannot enjoy on command.

Just an insight, he continues, *a very personal insight, a most honest confession of your character, not directly sexual if that is what you are thinking, be it that if you want, but as essential as that to your nature. You are primarily a nostalgic being,* says he, *you always bring up the past as if you want to return to it. To life and love as it was. Yet you bring up thinking in eternity in the very same breath.*

Yes, I am an historian of love. And therein lies the truth. The truth is eternal and thinking it makes you eternal.

Looking back is always a weakness, he says. *Backward looking is backwardness. Do you want to be a simpleton? You'll end up in the madhouse with a bad case of the stares. Be for the now I say. The now as it were, as you say.*

The simpleton would only see it that way. Backward looking is forwardness. Boldness. The man with no history has no future. I seek to retrieve the truth of a thing. In the temporal instances, something eternal. Something on the horizon of history that is not history, that which allows us to see beyond our tragic souls, to where we toss our spears into the void. One thing you are right about is that love is at the root of it. The reacquaintance of a beautiful idea with the idea of one's self. This is where personal power lies.

Now it's beauty. And power.

Shall I continue?

That's what you summoned me here for is it not?

No summons. You came freely in your new togs.

Well, I'm listening freely.

You have to be doubly attentive. Temporal connections are not the thing. Not the psychological. Logical connections are. Follow the necessary idea.

Any specific idea?

You'll know it when you think it.

Don't be cruel to me.

I will. I want you to know me. You want to know me, but to know me you'll have to know my idea. A clue before I start. The truth needs no sign. Failure is guaranteed if you follow the false trail of facts.

Listening—who listens? The speaker who is also the hearer prior to any audience. A listener unto himself. Next, our linguistic relations. *Friends, Romans and countrymen, lend me your ears.* The moment you listen, as much as the moment you speak, is the very moment you begin to know yourself, and knowing yourself is the selfsame moment of knowing others around you.

Listen to me and you'll know me, I tell him. I want to possess him as much as I possess the ideas I express to him in words. I want him to take what he hears as if it is said in his very own voice. He will take my words and speak them to himself. That is listening. At the same time I want to see him in a state of conversion, displaying the moments of this listening on his face, and in his body. Ditch the mother's manners.

When did this withdrawal of yours start? he asks.

At some point I felt the powerful pull of history, the tug of the personal past. So I marched back armed with the future. To commit the metaphysical murder.

Go on, tell me more, you are in good form, he says. *If you are going to dredge up the past, what of...*

Just listen! I cut him off because I don't want him to set the agenda. He is excited but I tell him not to be. It may not be exactly what he wants to hear. But he insists, spitting out lumps of the champ to make room for the words.

What of the bakery? he continues. *What of the mother? What of the humiliated old Fenian Shubert? What of murder and mayhem? What of sweet smelling young women? What of God? What of the activities in the orange haze, what of...?*

Dup! You can see the way his mind works. The name, indicative of a form. That is his anchor. He shall have it all, but in my order. In my time.

I can almost see that it's a case for the compensatory authorities?

The custodians of constabulary could never be involved. They wouldn't know which way to turn.

They don't want to hear it? Are they not after depravities as much as they once were not in the day of the cunt?

Dup! He had to be silenced, he was jacking me up trying to expose my underbelly.

The Fenian Irish name Seamus McGladdery hasn't worked for me for forty three years. It has worked against me. From the outset I needed a name that was not a betrayal.

Finally, I opted for intuition as the intuition avoided the interference of the abstraction. What intuition exactly? *One idea with its accompanying emotional effect can only be overcome by another more powerful one.* Carried along, sucked up, by a pure, unaffected capacity, into that realm of deliverance, I suddenly knew it and believed it to be not only true, but appropriate to a specific circumstance. What is at work here is the divine affect. An idea is nothing without an emotion, the thing that takes the body and the body of thought directly to its object. It then takes the object into itself, preserving it or overwhelming it.

He wants clarification. *Give me something I can grasp in my own simple language.* He claims a language of his own. A simple one. A follower of the absurd notion that there was some individual who was first to take part in a team game. The man first to utter a word. The speaker without a listener.

Travel. It's no distance at all. It's right there. Just as you came to me. In fact it really demanded nothing of a journey. He isn't familiar with the domain of immanence. None of us are until we receive the flash attributable to univocity. His world, the world in general, is that of the eminent subject, the eminent form, the eminent essence. Of the eminent organisation. The binding eminent word. The eminent social contract. The pre-eminence of God.

Is it true, he said, *is all you will tell me true?* I was waiting for that.

We finish up the champ and I take him into my retreat to expand. A concrete area about eighteen feet by eight, enclosed by high fences. We need the air after such a heavy feast.

This is identical to mine, as far as yards go, he says in a rather odd exhibition of pride. *The very same down to the planted borders. And I don't say it's the same lightly. You don't have to visit mine if you have this very same nest. But this is your nest and that's the end of it.* He begins to examine every object, after which he points and says that it is the very same as his. This plant pot, that plant. *If I move that plant pot do you think there'll be a key under it?* Then on to the position and style of a decommissioned yard light high on the house wall. Old roof tiles stacked in a corner. And on and on pointing. He insists on doing this every time he comes here, as if he has not been here before, or he is like a child in the rudimentary but productive stage of learning, or he is genuinely never been here. His child-like qualities are all too evident. I tell him to stop pointing.

2.

The unheeding fly, I say as a large blue bottle lands on my bare arm. *There's a lesson.*

In the confines of our concrete space I look at the Listener and ponder his confusion, made splendidly manifest with his hands running through his hair straining the hefty strands. He continues to point with one hand and fiddle with his hair with the other. Hair. It always seemed to play its part in human success and failure. Samson. Heir to head hair. Cymotrichous brunettes. *There was a tuft just above the ear, hardened by dry blood,* I tell him.

Where? asks the Listener. As if he didn't know.

Blood blown from the temple. A cold barrel placed strategically. That's what he wanted to hear. The exciting stuff. He sees the pain.

It's a sensitive area, the hair above the ear. Old Casey, the primary school headmaster, would grab you there if you were fooling about. *Do you remember?* He'd have you on your tiptoes squealing for mercy. He took the tuft between his forefinger and thumb, wetted by his tongue before pinching, and up you went.

He once had me by the temple tuft and on my tiptoes because I hadn't read my book when I said I had. Below the hem of my school shorts my bare knees knocked up a bony tune. *He's on high heels hell,* the devil's bootlickers roared. My eyes watered and the rest of them in the class said I was crying but I wasn't, though I couldn't look them in the face for fear of breaking down to a weakling's gurn. Just the pain causes the watering, that particular pain, lifting the scalp itself. *Rubbish*, they said, *you're gurning like a wee girl. Away and get yourself a wee dress.* I had tufts aplenty. Dark weighty hair still sprouts from my skull, inherited from thick, wavy-haired ancestors. It sprouts so fast, in still moments I can almost feel it inching out. Like a persistent itch. Bilko the barber always said that I had beautifully thick hair as he lopped it off in big clumps. He held the cut clumps high to admire them. I could see the appreciation in his eyes. I could feel it in his fingers deep in my scalp. Then he dropped a clump from on high and I saw it limp and unattached on my lap.

The mother with her wavy perm, in her unwavering simplicity, had a prejudice against the bald pate. To her it indicated a naked perversity of character. She liked male head hair to be grown sweet girl-like long, liked to see the effect of natural waves and curls. She wanted men always to be innocent children. At the same time she despised the effeminate man. What is at the root of that idea? The root of the hair thing. Separate strands of meaning requiring an effort of mind. Not yet braided in a unitary sense. The ideas are flowing freely. The body tells me so. It swells and throbs in a break for freedom.

At every chance the mother combed my mane up and over with those stubby fingers of hers and then stood back to admire the result. A pleasure, yet the pleasure was tainted. I didn't want what the mother wanted. I soon wanted thin hair. Straight thin hair. Thin black hair with a silky shine. Like a red Indian. A Comanche, or a Crow, or a member of the stubborn Blackfoot tribe. I asked baldy Bilko the barber for a thin Indian cut, not knowing how to describe it, and he laughed. He told the old men waiting their turn on the barber's bench what I requested and they all laughed too. Then he slowly massaged my skull under the waves and winked at the old men.

Flies buzz about us in our retreat. Flies have a thing about hair. Especially the big blood-sucking bruiser that is the cleg fly. The phrase get *out of my hair* originates with flies seeking to embed themselves annoyingly in the thick thatch. Very recently, in my retreat, the locks have been allowed to lengthen. A nostalgic tribute to the mother maybe. Just maybe, but maybe more. What is to be noticed most about the fly is its unheedingness. Its persistence.

Look what they do to the poor, helpless cows in the field. They buzz and buzz endlessly into their ears, up their nostrils, and sit on their arse holes. And those daft cows do nothing save, after ages of irritation, twitch their skin and wave their tails ineffectually. In *National Geographic* I saw a glossy close-up of a beautiful young girl in some far flung fly infested land behaving like a cow, with flies all over her face, up her nostrils, on cracked lips, in the very crunchy corners of her large sleepy, diseased eyes. Her look was one of cow-like resignation. No doubt eventually she would wave her hand gently in their direction. But, I never saw it, and it would be to no avail, the damn flies would come straight back after a swift mad epicycle or two and land again just where they had been enjoying themselves in their own particular unheeding fly fashion. Yes, the irritating nature of the fly. Like the Irish namesake, the person who is fly. The person who liked to wheedle their way into your life just to take anything precious you had. They would hang around you waiting for their moment.

I grew up with fly boys all around me. Like John Brannan from the council flats. He always wanted to play in my house just to steal my toy soldiers. He hid them in his filthy grey hanky when he thought I wasn't looking. Like a filthy conjurer. The mother told Brannan's mother that her son was a fly worthless being. Shouted all over the street. Flies and hair. All so very perplexing.

What do you think is at work inside this hairy head of mine? I say to him. He shrugs. *Error. Falsity. Delusion,* I tell him. He nods. He thinks he knows about error. *He* is the error of my ways.

I have fallen into an abyss of blunder. I declare. *Blundered into blunder with the inaccuracy of a blunderbuss. The error of the image. The source of natural decline into anger, fear, despair, anxiety.*

You just seem to have no humour left inside you, he says.

Is it any wonder? My history.

What was that you said? He heard me whispering something to myself. I was suddenly aware that another visitor was expected. I had whispered her name, *Mistress Liana,* and was immediately alarmed, nervous, hoping he hadn't heard me. He cannot be here when she arrives.

What? My history is what I said. Nothing more.

I see. What of history then? Alan the Listener asks.

Henry Ford, now there is a man who loved history. I gather some composure.

He appears confused. *Bunk! Didn't he say that history was bunk? Ex post facto and all that.*

Yes, he did indeed say that, but no wonder, if history is understood only as matter of fact. It would be bunk, as there would be no history and no truth. How often do you hear it? We don't want all that reasoning, just tell us the facts! The truth for them is in yes and no and not the know. The understanding of the lawyer and the journalist. The truth is, there are no facts.

I've hardened myself to that world of matter of factness. My history. My troubled past? Do I deny it? I deny that I deny it. *Deny everything,* says Walter Matthau in *A Guide for the Married Man.* That's the way to get through life.

You are a conjurer of words, a composer, he says. *You are arrogant. A twister. A Jacob. A twistymacatha. Those are facts. And you always want to deny me as well. Fact.*

A twistymacatha? Where did you get that word from? That's the mother's word. It's my word. Given to me by my Ma. Hearing it coming from another mouth, as if it belonged to the world, makes me shudder. It gathers my anger. It does not belong with him, in his mind, coming from his lips. The mother has gone and it belongs now only to me. There's other words, I wonder does he know them too?

Who do you think you are? he says. *What right have you? Words do not belong to you. You seek to belittle us all.*

What? You people have no regard for words.

Us? You evade the world with words.

The world is words. No. I confront it as it is, it abides with me. Abide. *Fast falls the eventide. The darkness deepens.* Lord, he darkens his mood. I see it and I am responsible for it. The good and the bad. An ethic. I seek no external counsel, no *expert* of the mind, no assistance from friendly types, fully armed with every clichéd rationalisation, to get me back on reality road. I'd preferably not be on the road—especially their main road, their reality—at all, but wandering the interesting and diverse lanes back and forth, in circles if need be, knowing my boundaries with intimacy.

Are you happy? he says.

Oh shite! Being happy requires a whole lifetime, I say. *As does sadness. Aristotle's idea. It cannot be considered as meaningful in any less time than that. It cannot exist in any less time. Nothing can. There are moments of happiness as there are moments of music in a symphony, but the moments of music are not the same as other moments of music nor are they the same as the whole piece, they are moments unique to themselves. I have my moments, but the whole edifice of life has not yet been built.*

He is not at all happy with that.

I am contented, I say

Oh? It doesn't seem so.

Contented not to have happiness. Contented even to have sadness. You lock yourself away.

Not so. Just moved into a different world.

What nonsense! You cannot have this private existence.

Contented with the balance of things, I continue, *as I become more acquainted with the nature of sadness. I have pleasure in knowing my sadness. My one valuable, untradable, possession.*

What utter bunkum! Madness. Completely. Self pity gone crackers. What good are you, what good to society? Worthless. Sadness is madness and resistance.

He wants to make me suffer.

It is necessary. Bend to still necessity, says Nietzsche.

Ah fuck Nietzsche the mad fool. Was it necessary that he died a madman? That's where you are heading, as I said.

We must get sadder unless we remain children and we simply cannot. There is genius in a child, a genius which we soon smother with the meagre capacity of adulthood. You must be as children, says the Christian.

I don't think you answered my question.

Well, let's see, I haven't told you everything.

The Lord shall smite thee with madness, and blindness, and astonishment of heart.

Deuteronomy 28:28. I like to quote scripture to him but he's never impressed.

History must start with a concept. An idea, I tell him.

What idea?

An idea that in some way forms experience, that decides for us the way things are. One we know well. Madness.

I first encountered it in church when I was about ten, and it soon alerted me to the general madness. It came to me in a mad babble.

The language of mad Jacky B, the punch drunk old boxer. *Ooh-la-la-ma-na-na-lama-na-ooh-la-la.* A mad tongue, a meaningless babble that was transformed into some form of common sense. The holy ghost had given him the babble, and to someone else it had given the gift to interpret it. It was always a message of joy. He wore a green wig that didn't match his sparse natural fair hair, nor did it fit adequately, and some said he was simple, having been punched back to infancy in the boxing ring.

When the spirit moved so did he, leaving his seat to shadow spar up and down the church aisle, throwing jabs, uppercuts and hooks at the unseen demons that inhabited the air around him, hoping to land a knockout blow. This was a madness that scared me even more than the immature thoughts of ghosts. I imagined him at the end of the bed in the dark. The boxer and the saint he was to some, two courageous characters in one. And isn't that what we all are? Two in one. The one is always more.

But madness is thinking and living in circles and circles within circles, and circles orbiting other circles. So it was in Ulster. A place of Ptolemaic politics and madness. Mad Ulster epicycles in the otherthinking place. Quantity, five hundred, I said

What of it? said Alan.

More madness. 1972. The dead. The murdered. The mad, murderous and frightening year. Can you imagine it?

I think so. Right out of Jacky B's book of madness.

3.

Nineteen and seventy-two, as it is said there in that place of sayings and imaginings, by the makers of make-believe. Just like the old Israelites. The factory that is the Ulster mind, manufacturing dangerous, incendiary notions and idols. Black Belfast, a place of linguistic licence, dilemmas of the mind and the inner essence. A place of the crowd and the universal voice. The fact of Belfast. The old *Béal Feirste*, the mouth of the Farset, the wee farce of a river on which the city was built. The old river languishes in obscurity under the concrete of Bridge Street. The big built-up city now on the River Lagan that flows for all to see from the embankments and the towpaths that lead out to the countryside. The city of Antrim and Down that you can see in one big view standing on the grand Cave Hill behind it, looking out towards the eternally miserable Irish sea.

A miserable view for a miserable people. Alan was alert.

Nineteen and seventy-two. Five fucking hundred dead! Can you imagine it? A bloody vision. Out in the street, you had to look over your shoulder. Don't walk alone we're told. Bloody Sunday, the bent priest with his white hanky. Waving for a bit of peace. Bloody Friday, the bus station bodies shovelled up in black bin bags. Can you imagine it? Bloody hell! It's war. A vacuum in America—death sucking up Hoover and Truman. Watergate opening the naïve eyes. End of Apollo. Kissinger says, *Peace is at hand.* Black September. None of that. Nothing else existed but Ulster.

The Godfather, says Alan, alive to my alignment of thought.
Amazing grace.
The first time ever I saw your face.
Without you.
Alone again.
Imagine.
Don't let it die. Or say goodbye.
Who won the cup? I can't remember.

I was on a caravan site in Millisle County Down, sunbathing on a cloudy day, a fraction asleep, listening to Hurricane Smith on the radio. Don't let it die. I missed the cup.

Fuck sake! No one misses the cup.

There wasn't as much as one TV in Millisle. Not so much as a wave in the sea. Make your own fun was the saying going about. It was a dead place was another saying. Old folk just staring out at the waveless sea.

Back to the old city. By a thumb along a narrow country lane. How did I know it? The wonder of wounded Johnny McQueen in *Odd Man Out,* staggering around its dismal streets. *That was a city and a half,* said the father who knew infinity by saying the same things endlessly. 'Twas a city that people built out of no particular purpose but many purposes, great and small and some particularly stupid. If you thought seriously and single-mindedly about life and the shortness of it you'd never build a thing like this. You'd live for the present. In a place like Millisle. Nobody would ever see what they foresaw. But they did it anyway here as elsewhere and it grew with everything that is blind, ambition, thrift, invention, but blind as a bat is blind. They could see in the dark, like a blind man can see colours. Designs from elsewhere were grafted onto the Lagan valley by the steel hard men of the Industrial Revolution, inspired by their practical Victorian minds. *They* found themselves in facts. The fact of work, the fact of power, power that made the fact of wealth. But wealth was not everything, nor was it nothing. It could never turn heads away from tradition and culture sufficiently. It was a city not of one dream but of many that were, in their way of accumulation, the raw material of future nightmares.

And then there was the deeper paradox, the sheer contradiction of the place that emerged out of facts. Those who claimed cleanliness were dirty, the humble were arrogant, the kind were cruel, the intelligent were ignorant, the beautiful were ugly, those who should have spoken were silent, those who endlessly shouted should have listened, those who claimed to be peaceful were war mongers, and most hideous of all, those who claimed courage were cowards.

Do you remember the day?

What day?

That Friday?

Good Friday?

Bloody good Friday.

Bloody do. That was madness alright. Madness right up there with Jesus on the cross.

There was courage with Christ, here there was only cowardice. Courage disappeared down the sewers and up the back entries. Out came the gangs of butchers thinking that all was permitted. Did you ever hear tell of old slabbery McGowan? Now there's a tale to tell of buses and bombs.

Five-thirty p.m. or thereabouts on that Thursday evening. Old slabbery mouth McGowan, the man himself so he thought, stood at this dusky moment outside his own Belfast front door, a few doors down from us, surveying street life. Actually, not his own front door at all, the house was rented, but McGowan knew that it could have been his, had he so chosen. That then was good enough for him, for in declining to make it his inspired a feeling of authority, it made him feel that he was in control of his destiny.

His invitational sleazy grin and wanton lips marked him out as a possible degenerate. Children from the houses round and about played joyously low in his orbit but his degeneracy was to them, as yet, an invisible thing. So, there he stood in his vast, stained vest reflecting upon the enjoyments he desired and the most recent desires that had been enjoyed. He always appeared to have just emptied a mammoth meal into his gut, routinely feeling with his greasy hands the splendid fullness of his belly held in the exposed tight string vest. He was aware of his status as a desiring being, only wanting to do what he enjoyed, and was grateful he was not a being which had no wants, a dead being, or a living being like a flower.

As the sun set on his day, his thought was for a particular tomorrow. He would take himself on a bus trip out of town. It would be a pleasant change from life in the increasingly dangerous city. He saw himself rising with the sun and setting out on foot under a clear blue sky to the bus station, buying his return ticket and boarding the bus. He foresaw and felt the delightful slow pace of the journey and the agreeable company of other happy day-trippers seeing the back of badness, barricades and bombs. He congratulated himself on his ability to see himself in the tomorrow in so many ways, clear as day, just as the weatherman could see the course of the weather.

So, it happened as McGowan foresaw. He rose with the sun. He ate a large fried breakfast. He walked under a clear blue sky to the bus station. He bought his return ticket. The bus duly arrived. He placed a foot forward to board, but he boarded not, for he was, with that raised foot, exploded in an instant, all of him, into eternity.

Old McGowan was part of someone else's desire. And the world was not to know his degeneracy. Nor would he experience the full extent of it. We experienced the full extent of it in laughter. His vast vest blown off him, landing in someone's back garden. His bubbling saliva hitting the back of someone's nut.

What a laugh we thought it was! said Alan the Listener. *His body bits could have been put straight on to the butcher's slab.*

There's no end to what you can laugh at here, I replied.

That's the mad Ulster people for you.

Ha! Have you heard of the British Israelites? That's who the Protestants think they are. A chosen people after the Jews. And Ptolemy the astronomer, have you heard of him? His followers were like a circus act, circuitous, the masters of the epicycle. By adding more and more circles they thought they could explain the geocentric astronomy. Every time a problem arose with the movements of the planets in went another circle. They went mad with the circles, just like the Ulster politics does. And that is where the madness resides. Circular thinking and endless additional circles to make you dizzy. And the mad marching. Does any nation march as much as the Ulster nation? They should build a circular road around Belfast and then they could march to their heart's content.

But here's a thing to note. The marching is a form of cowardice. Beware the crowd, said Seneca. And, the crowd is untruth, said Kierkegaard. They always need witnesses to their acts. They do everything collectively. Far from the act of the soul. Here nobility is non-existent. The marching mob risks nothing, the gangs of butchers risk nothing, and so each member of the marching mob and the gang is submissive, and therefore a coward. So, the Ulster people know what they know and do not want to know any more. That is why I hide myself away. Alan the Listener says nothing and shows nothing. Is he listening?

4.

The five-thirty p.m. time was significant. The time of tension, a brute of a time, a reminder of a particular extension, urging intuitions and direction, the time I loathed was always the time that came too quickly.

I expected McGowan would be outside his door as usual and all then would be as usual. The humour of the day had subsided. Football in the entry finished and friends had gone their own ways. Duration prevailed over time on that quick-to-darkness November Friday evening. No more hoping that God would mark this moment and make time stand still or that the holy rapture would arrive sooner than expected. An intuition of something immediately unpleasant was always upon me in these moments. I hoisted my reluctant, boyish arse from the old, unevenly unsprung brown settee and headed for work.

Upon standing, I faced myself in the grand old mirror weighing heavily on the slate mantelpiece. I pulled the sweat-stuck corduroy pants out of my backside as I stood and stared. That mirror! I detested seeing myself at this time. What did I see? Nothing of joy. Pure pity. Turning away and looking through the bay window I saw it was another dirty Belfast dusk with nothing by way of a pleasant sensation to entice the soul outside. The rain was on its way. There was no remedy for the close dampness that was an almost permanent feature of the November weather.

The pulp I chewed was the dinner I had eaten about half an hour before. Pulp of fried eggs, bacon and soda bread. I couldn't swallow, such was the dryness of my mouth and the narrowing of the throat. I moved my light frame with a familiar heaviness, accompanied by weighty and burdensome ideas. I left by the back door, located in the kitchen, as usual, walked through the yard, turned right after exiting the yard door, walked a short distance up the entry, turned right and right again to pass my own front door, all as usual. Why didn't I just leave by the front door? It was a routine I had adopted since leaving school the previous summer, maybe because I wanted to leave with a more recent memory of the entry. What was not as usual was that the man McGowan wasn't there as expected outside his door. What cruel contingency, then, awaited, in a place and time that seemed governed by necessity?

I shuffled on after a brief pause to take in McGowan's absence and took the same extended route as usual. I considered another one, just for the change, but for no known reason decided against it. There was, however, a good reason to take the alternative route. You would most likely avoid a firm army frisking up against a wall, or in a dark doorway, being booted about if your body language wasn't sufficiently appeasing to the soldiers.

It was a fifteen minute walk at my usual lazy and drowsy pace, out of the pleasant Victorian tree-lined avenues where I lived, destined for the miserable Markets area. In between I passed through a variety of encircling slums of cramped and dismal digs. The rain came as half-expected, hardly detectable as drops, lashing everything in sight, blinding the eyes that looked for a destination. I passed the gasworks, with its ghastly aroma of smelted coke climbing up and over those high red brick walls, mixing down with the rain into the nostrils of the working population returning home in their droves to their warm dinners, to their fondling families, to their cosy evenings in.

Mostly I thought of the body. My tight little torso. Terribly attractive. My body in its own relation. And other bodies all around that were in their own relation also. Soon enough I encountered an army patrol, at the beginning of Cromac Street, a few streets away from work. I was frisked with several other men heading in my direction. Due to the saturated state of our clothes we were given only a brisk light frisk against the gasworks' walls, and allowed to pass on through to the Markets. In these final few yards I was aware of simple body processes, the steps I took, my teeth still biting down onto the pulp in my mouth, an itch on my neck, an open sweaty palm, all of which created a sense of momentary calm. If I thought at all in abstraction from the body, I would think of home. I would undoubtedly think of McGowan's absence, then the presence of homely things. Things that were necessary to know in order to know me.

Rising up before me when I turned that final corner were the immense factory gates. They were the gates of Hell, remote from saintly and noble notions. Yet, I was bent and bowed as I approached, as if out of reverence. It was in fact shame as I breezed past those agitated souls, the jobbers, young and old, who stamped their freezing feet in the damp all day long, and drew breath on their thin, self-rolled fags, hopeful and desperate for a night's human labour. I entered like a coward with my head dipped down and hidden into my jacket, but sometimes I tried to think of myself as a gut-wounded warrior.

Yes, they knew me mainly as foreman Frank McGladdery's son, and knew the advantage I had over their chances of getting work, yet they stood there stoically without hate or a sign of envy or hostility. But, I was never to be one of them. I simply stole in and stole out and stole their work. When they did get in for a night's labour they even offered me a form of friendship. I felt guilty, but they deserved to have that affect upon me, at the very least.

The bakery was a vast effort in complexity. Architectural and interactive. To stand in it, without a consciousness of its function, was to know the tragedy of Man naturalised, weakened in the midst of the mechanical. Unless, in a further act, a man could animate unknown capacities, strip down his formal boundaries, to associate with the fiery furnaces, the ovens, the oiled cogs and wheels, the conveyer belts, the roaring lorries, the cold empty spaces, the bogies, to ride the electric ponies, in such a way as to know it as affective effort. It was also the huge beast of a building in the midst of that maze of grimy cobbled streets where Man, removed from Nature, moved in sadness.

The Markets nominally. Real markets there once were, owned once by the aristocratic marvel that was the Marquis of Donegal, but no more. Seeking to maximise his power in death, however, he left his mark in the form of the feminisation of thoroughfares. The adjoining streets around the area were named after his daughters, Eliza Street, Catherine Street, Joy Street, Charlotte Street, Henrietta Street, Grace Street, May Street.

Following a narrow corridor, to the side of the main gate, I arrived at the time office. At a small window I was greeted by Joseph Lundy, the timekeeper. I only knew him as an upper body. His head, shoulders and upper chest only, framed by the high window at which he appeared when you rang a bell. I had yet to see him in his total corporeal glory. A perfect job for a man without legs. The idea of a legless man scared me. A dirty legless man even more. A legless coalman with his angry black face and grasping black hands. With wheels on his stumps to move him along swiftly to catch you. Coming across a legless man like this under a dim gas light, or emerging from the deep shadows, supplied me with sufficient formal and material stuff to know the meaning of fear. The particular of fear.

This little official realm was Lundy the timekeeper's holy of holies. His legless arse sliding about on a mercy seat. The impenetrable haze to his rear was the pillar of smoke that by day shrouded the important men who entered by a private side door. The men with the coloured collars on their long white doctor's coats. Or more rarely, the men with expensive suits and shiny shoes which, in their confident step, announced a force. Lundy was a servant of servants to the high priests of the place, but he was also the high priest of signatures. He commanded the lower ranks who appeared at his window to sign his book, the book veiled with dirt and grease and held together with tight elastic bands. He placed his greasy forefinger in the empty space you had to sign. When it was removed there was a new grease stain. The ink slipped over the grease. I had to press firmly with Lundy's very own slippery pen. I could see how all this gave him a strong sense of himself as a meaningful man.

Ah, Frank McGladdery's son, he'd always shout, delivering the line to the ears of those waiting at the gate.

In exchange for our scribbled signatures we received laundered and pressed, loose-fitting heavy cotton whites, which consisted of a short sleeved top and wide ill-fitting pants, both usually worn over our bare bodies, such was the heat of the place. From time to time I considered them as robes of holy araiment. Holding the whites in their folded form in both arms, I moved out of the time office corridor leaving the legless Lundy behind. *Get behind me legless Lundy,* I whispered.

With purpose I walked through the vast, cold yards, past the lorry loading bays, slipping beyond the busy checkers, long ticket rolls in hand checking their extensive orders, then through the fancy room, with its stacked trays of sweet iced buns and cream cakes. I followed the smell of freshly baked bread of every sort to the belt room, where I'd be assigned a job of work for the night, where the heat hit with considerable force.

In his minuscule mousehole of an office at the corner of the room of bread conveyer belts I encountered the broody and moody and abrupt Jimmy McClair, the belt room boss. Charge-hand was the official title, the hand that was thick and strong with bulging veins and always waving about to accompany this or that verbal command. A long, white coat with a green collar marked out his higher status. He could be funny but only ever funny in his favour, never at his expense. The last word was always with him, a hit and run comedian. A comic terrorist. But under the bad breath and behind his back he was mockingly called Chocolate Éclair, not just because the names fitted snugly together, but because he had migrated from the sweet domain of the pastry rooms. That he was a wanker was the general opinion. A Protestant wanker at that, ruling over a Fenian workforce.

He was a wanker, said Alan.

You knew him?

I can tell.

McClair assigned me to the bastard batch, the hottest, hardest bastard of a job in the place. The regular batch man never turned in on a Friday night, he was so exhausted. The batch chain was close to Jimmy Éclair's office, near the front wall of the belt room, always under his misty, wandering-eyed scrutiny. It consisted of wire trays of steaming, uncut loaves on a never-ending chain that circulated from the top of the building, where the bakers loaded it up after baking, to the bottom, where the batchman plucked the trays off and slid them into the slots of wheeled bogies behind him.

The heat coming off the steaming loaves was transferred to the wire trays, so they burnt the inner arms when they were lifted, and the sharp jutting edges of the battered and bent wires cut into the skin and opened up the flesh. But the process itself—lifting the weighty wire trays, twisting round, depositing them, twisting back, lifting again—was perfect exercise for the body and, to a certain extent the mind. I could feel my shoulders and upper arms harden and the stomach tightening to a permanent firm muscle through every hour of every shift.

Weight loss was inevitable, the body endlessly perspiring. The reduction was on display in my hollow, high cheeks, and a well withdrawn abdomen. This, together with the express rate at which I worked the chain, earned me the affectionate nickname, the greyhound. And its affects were good, as they found their origins in me. *It'll make a man of you,* said Éclair. *The batch isn't for a wee bitch. And for fuck's sake don't fuck it up. Don't anger the fucking bakers up there in their floury fucking heaven.*

The bakers who sent the newly batch loaves down to be sliced and wrapped hated to see it coming back up as it occupied the space for more to be sent down. They were Gods up in their floury heaven, and their wrath was great. Contingency, however, abounded. As the bakers depended on me, so I depended on the bogie men to supply empty bogies for the batch trays, and the bogie men depended on the lorries returning on time from their deliveries with empty bogies. The whole process was as circular as the batch chain itself. Bogies were also needed for the packers, the checkers and the belt men, and a short supply of bogies meant chaos.

It occurred to me at some point shortly after starting the shift that that to master this task would be a great achievement. To master anything, and not be mastered.

The linguistic constitution of the place was governed by the inability to be acquainted with what was questionable. Like the idea of manhood, which often specified the whole bloated individual and collective consciousness. Related to it was a fake form of fortitude, a dedication to uncleanness, and a cultivation of the crude, the brutish and the uncouth. With their tired arses parked on wooden benches in the locker room where I saw them collectively, they shouted outrageous claims to virility loudly and without fear in each other's faces, produced their wank weary cocks to simulate the business of sex, and stank from every puny pore.

Dirty skitters, the mother would say in her madness.

I sometimes wished I could cultivate an appropriate crudeness that would fit in with theirs, just for those occasions, but I only ever remained a sweet smiling boy among brutes.

Then there was the man McGraw.

Magic, mastery and McGraw. McGraw the mystery man and McGraw's private world made known. How to master it? The question of mastery arose for the first time. How to master myself? How to master his hand of friendship. His body. His affects. What of my affects upon him? My body as his consciousness. How to master the batch chain depended on being a master of McGraw's constant stare from across the belt room. He mastered his own work, whilst keeping his eyes firmly fixed on me. What is it exactly to master a thing? Something magical. Not the spells and such primitive notions to control nature prevalent in the abusive understanding of magic, but knowing a technique. Knowing the secrets to the ways in which we distribute ourselves with a degree of power. The ceremonies, the rituals. What were McGraw's secrets? To know this would mean going through a painful process of getting to know McGraw and allowing him to know me.

His interest in me gathered momentum the minute I entered into his field of epistemic vision. He wanted to know me and made himself immediately available to me to know. So, he presented himself, or perhaps exhibited himself. And what did I see? Of the form that was his body I saw a sick man. A diseased devil. A poisoned snake. Was the man dying? How could such decay be associated with health? Was he dying, or merely striving in other ways?

Once he knew my ritual tastes there was very little restraint to his eagerness to offer himself up to me in words as an innocent victim of working class cultural brutality, membership of which he tried to erase by flirting with items of accessible culture. Accessible mainly by mail order from the Sunday newspapers, collections of the popular classics in music and literature. Here he found a common ground with me, the ground on which to build.

In my first few weeks McGraw showered me with gifts of books and records. He nominated himself to show me the way of things, easing himself into unpleasantly close proximity on my first day. Jimmy Éclair was wondering where to put me. McGraw knew and gave me his powerful meaty hand to shake. In its grip was the transmission of all his vices. I didn't yet know their form, only the unformed, immanent, intense, anonymous bodily force that occupies you and shakes you up to what is called an intuition. Or a feeling. In animal terms, an instinct. A mapping of something that, in its particular (of particles) way strives to associate or dissociate, friendly or hostile in its affect and not yet in the definitive form.

Out of his mouth came the language of decomposition and decline, an expression meant to be impressive and uplifting but it was in truth grounded in desperation. He was fighting his final battles to find his form, but fighting on two fronts. What preserved him here in the workplace, and allowed him to ease himself around his social equals, was a weakening capacity to be unrefined, while his half enlightened ideas, exclusive to me, roped in my youthful dissidence.

This, for me, was at first a welcomed anchor in a rough sea, for the titanic anchor would soon become an intolerable weight, holding me in place and then dragging me down into a dark and dangerous turbulence.

The dayshift would spill out of the locker room at six p.m. destined for the boozers in the streets around the bakery. The night shift would spill out of the boozers destined for the locker room, to get ready to populate the floors of the various rooms before the machinery started up again and for the bread to flow.

In my clean whites I would take my stand at the chain and wait for it to circulate. Across the room, at the far side, was McGraw in plain view. In this quiet unmoving moment he gave me his best stares. When the conveyer belts started he lifted the loaves and placed them in trays with mechanical grabber accuracy but rarely diverted his eyes from me.

The break times were staggered, often leaving McGraw and me alone together in the belt room, the critical process of befriending was set in motion. Whatever the actual status of cultural matters in the McGraw mind, he soon dispensed with the need to use them as preliminaries in our conversations. This decline of ordinary discourse was gradual. With equal slowness he introduced wordless expressions, modes of bodily movement that initially seemed to have no connection with anything. When they substituted everything that was meaningful I intended to them with a high degree of uncertainty.

Off he went with his lips. His fingers and his hips. His straightened forefinger would pass over his pouted lips, then would be inserted into a small opening he made in them, his eyes falling and rising in their sockets. He looked down at the floor and then up at me and smiled in a simplistic way. Like a backward idiot. His tongue tip would rest upon the middle of his upper lip and work its way along from side to side. He rested a hand delicately on his sidewardly extended hip, then moved it slowly onto his upper thigh with his fingers splayed. Then the splayed fingers were ruminating inside his roomy white leggings. A combination of these acts then became routine. These mannerisms were specially reserved for closer encounters except the pouting lips that would be administered from the distance between his bread belt and my batch chain.

What was he doing? Asks Alan.

Don't you know? He was striving. Sticky was striving.

Sticky?

The father said he knew him as Sticky McGraw when he was young.

Striving Sticky. Was he striving then?

Apparently so, he had no friends and he stuck around where he wasn't wanted just to show he had friends. The father said he was a spoilt huffy puffy. When he didn't get what he wanted he blew his horn. Alan cracked up laughing. We both did. *And then the father and his friends would debag him. He'd be happy to be humbled just to mooch along with everyone.*

There's nothing funnier than a good debagging, especially on a spoilt fat cunt.

It didn't end there. After they debagged him they chucked his trousers down a sewer pipe and had him playing a blind Bart in a brutal blind man's buff. With his legs and arse in the buff he'd be shoved against walls, kicked and punched in an unrestrained fashion. What a laugh!

The wants were upon me. The wants that never waned nor withered. The desiderium of wants. The longing for more wants. And soon the wants specified the direction and the object, the only ways to satisfy the wants. The actions were specified for each want. My wants of body, the craving wants of emotions. Fear wanting aversion and avoidance, shame, the desire to conceal. The body wants prevailed, they required fondling and caressing and the McGraw movements soon became meaningful. The seedy seduction, coming at me from behind whilst I was occupied with the demands of the relentless chain. In idle moments his tender touches triumphed. And then the unthinkable, less fear at his approaches, less avoidance, less shame and guilt and less concealment. With the wants in control, the specified object became McGraw, but only the idea of McGraw, the idea of an acting McGraw. I never offered myself up to him actively, never responded in kind to his advances, as his decaying body was offensive to me. My stiffening body was my resistance, I never used my lips, my hands or my hips. But McGraw never saw past me, I was his immediate future.

I looked at the clock behind me. It was only seven p.m. Another eleven hours of resistance. There he went. McGraw withdrew and wandered back to his belt as the others returned from their break. And there he was, there as himself staring at me. There and there as...

5.

Thereness and thereness as. The feminine force. Alan gave me his poem to read. Despite his defiant cynicism over fancy words he had been secretly scribbling.

There is the *there*
the *just there*
And, there is the *there as*
The *there as* something

To be *just there*
Bare of outward impact
With nothing to share
A mere fact

To be *there as*
Is a power to share
The inner with the outer
A virtuous snare

Desire, desire, desire, the mother desired something, but knew not what. Neither did the rest of us. If she yearned for love, there was no way it could be given. She was unlovable in her quagmire of desire. So, earlier in the day, before I set off for work, she had been carted away from the home and taken to the Shaftesbury Street

Mental Hospital, just as she had been many a time before. One minute she was there, sitting there as quietly in her chair, then she wasn't there, but elsewhere, *there as* a lunatic. When she came back weeks later, she wasn't *there* or *there as* anything.

Her obsession was with the *thereness* or the *thereness as* of being, an insight that drove her mad. As I sat waiting for the clock to tick around to five-thirty p.m., with her absence in mind, I felt unbearably sad. And with the need to be elsewhere something of a state of panic surfaced.

For her, it would all commence with an unstoppable rush of impatience for the father to be there, there in the home. He was elsewhere, and his absence sent her imagination into convulsions. What was he doing elsewhere?

There he is! she would declare, as the father came in through the door. *There he is, there he stands, there he looks the image of innocence.* Then the *there as. There he is, there as the big manager, there he is there as the gentleman. There he is, there as the destroyer of my life.* His initial silence was prodigious. It set her off on the trail insults, the unleashing of the louse idiom.

There is the louse. The bloody louse. Sitting there, you're not even a lowly louse. More like a wee squeaky mouse. A louse messing up my house. What do you think you are? you louse, a louse in a suit who thinks he's a big manager in a big house. Big, big big manager. But, ah ha, you're nothing, nothing, nothing but a louse. A manager louse, a lousy manager. You come from a family of louses but you are the biggest louse of all. The louse of all bloody louses. Once a louse always a louse. No! A louse is too good for you. You're not even a bloody louse. You're lower than the louse. I married someone lower than a louse!

Oh, the poetic power of it!

When he responded it was with relative economy and irritating reason and restraint and sometimes even with a smile. *Aye you'd know about lice, and lice it is. Plural. Your family, the whole menagerie*

*of them were born like lice and slept with the lice. A filthy lot living
in shite and lice and the shite of lice. You are talking as an authority
on lice because your whole family are intimate with lice. You are the
descendants of lice, all similar to lice the lice probably think your lot are
just the same as them. Did you ever hear of liceland? The plague of lice
in ancient Egypt is where your ancestors were from—that is where
your relations come from. Gypsy lice.*

Unable to stem her own enthusiasm for the insult, she quickly
interrupted his flow with a savage shout, full to the brim with spite.

You are a louse! she continued. *You're a twister. You should have
been called Jacob because you are a twister. You have the wrong name.
You're a louse, a bloody big louse! Jacob Louse, that's a good name for
you. Take your filthy lousy body out of my sight—just get out of my sight.*

I'm not going anywhere.

No, it was she who was going somewhere.

In Great Shaftesbury Street Hospital, the great medical
temple of mind healing, they used all the crude weapons at their
disposal to find the remedy for *thereness* and *thereness as*. The blunt
psychological treatment tools yielded little and the chemical-
electrical approach over a two- or three-week period sent us back
a marvellously mild-mannered woman but not *the* woman. It was
yet another woman. A medical marvel of a woman with nothing
to say.

6.

Little houses, housing their secrets. Continuous filth. Filthy secrets. Upright coffins, interring the living, choking them out of life. The stench of death and dying. All badness met in the Market streets. How do you get to know anything worthwhile in a place like this? Before you die. Reared by ignorance. Obeying the obedient. How does it happen that you throw off habitual knowledge and finally know what something means? Not in the single eureka moment. How is it, for instance, at what point is it, that you turn and stand your ground against injustice?

When I took my first break I took it alone. McGraw, who had still to take his, had to wait to be subbed as there was no one available. That was a brief relief. Éclair told me to go and shoved Malachi Sloane, one of the bogie men, into my place. I had worked out a strategy for a smooth takeover, I didn't want Malachi to mess it up for me, but I could see the fear in his eyes as he struggled to lift the first wire tray off the chain.

I walked through the dark tunnel out of the warm belt room and into the cold, cavernous yards heading for the concrete stairs to the canteen. The night checkers, who were usually there in the yards filling up their orders, were unaccountably absent. It was the first inkling I had that matters outside were escalating into something new and nasty.

The canteen was, as expected, whisper quiet, just what I wanted for a few minutes. On the dayshift this wouldn't have been possible, with hundreds of whited workers riotously enjoying their greasy nourishment and devouring the silence.

Old Lanny, the night supervisor, was behind his counter full of anticipation for a catering encounter. Lanny didn't like me, I was too much of a child to him and he declared time and time again his hatred for kids. *Even when I was a kid,* he said, *I hated all the other kids.* I ordered my usual, a glass of ice cold milk—to settle my nervous stomach—and a ham sandwich, but Lanny was keen for my ear and to impress me with a prophesy.

There's going to be hell to pay for someone tonight, he growled. Someone'll pay the fucking price.

For who? I said.

For anyone. They'll want a scapegoat.

Who?

Anyone. Whoever is at it outside. The army will shoot somebody, anybody, and say they had a gun on them. They won't discriminate. And those fly Provo boys, they'll see to you as soon as fart or take a shite. And they're on the physic those boys with guns in their hands. So watch yourself.

But what's going on?

No idea, but it's in the air. In the air when I walked through those gates. Seen it all before.

Most of the time old Lanny needed healing in the head. Evangelical healing to take the nonsense out of him. Much like the mother. Everyone called him an old woman. *Away and wear a wee girl's dress,* they'd say. His full name was Lanny Mustgrave. Every time I saw him I thought he looked that bit closer to his grave. No less so this time. Maybe this would be his night.

He always had the black brew in, or close to, his hand. Old Stewed tea without milk that looked like crude oil. He was bent almost at right angles due to some spinal problem and he also had a limp. In his bent state he had to cock his neck and move his eyeballs to the upper edges of his sockets to get you in his sights. He needed evangelical healing of the body as well.

He wore slippers and felt more at home at work than at home. The hideous general odour of his home life, related in some respect to a rotting green root vegetable, accompanied him to work. Going about the duties, that implied at least an elementary awareness of the forms of contamination, he picked his nose and scratched his arse with vigour.

Lanny was a man with a sceptical amplitude that was hard to ignore. His mind was a twisted as his body, his world never straight. His language was almost as primary as a child prior to the phase of special productivity. He darted in and out of general communication, most of his utterances unaddressed even to himself. Then addressed only to himself, but how much he listened was hard to tell. And finally, in a partial awareness of others about him, there were the utterances that might have been interpreted by another man as being spoken to him. Here he was a carnaptious cunt in the language of the ordinary man.

With me he desired superiority, mostly with a loud voice that was intended as much for other ears as it was for mine. Here, I thought, was a man with a genuine theological gripe. Inheriting a twisted stature which forced his face to point always to hell, to live a life endlessly mocked by the upright in his community, it was reasonable for him, as an impoverished expression of humanity, to try to extend his limited power and make himself greater than God, by proclaiming that he existed and God did not. He was ready to declare God's non-existence by and through *his* very existence.

So that's the thing to be, an atheist. An unfearing person. You just have to look at me and ask, what have I to fear? And, what do I thank him for? What do I worship him for?

I listened and gave him my interested gaze for free which I thought he hardly deserved. His definition of an atheist as an unfearing person was a wonder of an idea coming from him. Of course I wasn't able to tell him that atheism was not rejecting the idea of God, but *an* idea of God. Only the God who is a tyrant, or a judge, a God of love, a God who provides. And of course the idea of a God-fearing person fits into that model. I was also unable to explain to him deism, or pantheism. I was unable to advance his knowledge of the world religions. It was Lanny, and his like who inspired me to such learning. I couldn't tell him that to be a Buddhist was to be an atheist. But I could imagine what he would say. *Ah, the Buddhism, yes, how could God be everything, for fuck sake? The Buddhism is just another word for bullshite. If God was everything he would be bullshite as well. The God of bullshite. And he'd be the God of the bullshite coming from your mouth. Sure what do they know in their misery and poverty and pain the poor stupid creatures? No wonder they came up with a buck stupid idea like that. They haven't the brains of fully fed people with no pain, if they had the brains they would see that there couldn't be a God if they were living like they were in hot hell of a country that boils their brains to ignorance.*

What he did say to my silence came as a surprise. *But you are a Protestant, young McGladdery. Maybe you and your Da and Ma have found the best way to deal with a missing God. Invent a new one, eh?*

I was unsure what he meant by that remark, but in time it came to me. The rewards for being a Protestant seemed greater. All the bosses in the bakery were Protestants, the workers all Catholic.

When I studied him I saw that his body, not as impotent as he thought, told him about God. His starting point was that interaction of his tortured torso with the world. In every aching joint, in every moment that he moved a muscle, or looked at the unfair world of upright bodies, there was a testimony to the absence of God, and the presence only of forces adequate or inadequate to a task. A purely practical world.

My older brother Frankie Jr., older and theologically wiser, told me that men like Lanny were mere epistemic illusions in a bigger metaphysical picture. That Lanny himself was living in an anguished consciousness that led to a condemnation of all that was true. Whether they believed in God or not mattered little, they all lived in and through an illusion. The bad that Lanny saw in his body was not really bad, and his sadness was not really sad.

It is as it is, is the old Islamic philosophical formula, said Frankie Jr.

Lanny wasn't finished, however. *The men who went to the moon saw not a sign of his divine majesty. Nothing there but rocks and soil and dark all around. Not a soul, just soil. Not even a drop of water to feed a single wee flower. Not a sign of his Lordship or even an angel in sight. Not a whiff or a swirl of a spirit. So, what do you say to that, son?*

I said nothing, but I loved his expression: *a whiff or a swirl of a spirit.* That was nice and I noted it, but I didn't tell him. Constrained in his crookedness he was unable to look me in the eye. *It's a fact. So you can't argue with science now can you. It's a fact, a scientific fact. You can't argue with a fact from science. A fact's a fact's an effing fact,* he drummed on.

The philosopher Karl Jaspers wrote: *What a man comes to be depends on whatever God he envisages in his faith… whatever God a man sees will create his humanity.* Where did that leave Lanny? The poverty of his being, of his humanity was reflected perfectly in the emptiness of his idea of God. It was so poorly defined it was nothing. He was nothing. I immediately thought of the verse in Matthew's Gospel: *Ye are the salt of the earth, but if the salt has lost its savour, with what shall it be salted? It is thereafter good for nothing but to be cast out, and be trodden underfoot of men.* Lanny's God had lost its savour, and was good for nothing.

Listen Lanny…

Ah, what the fuck does it matter anyway? What difference does it all make? he protested angrily.

All was then silence. And the silence led me to hearing my own body once again. All inside and no outside.

There it is, did you hear it? I heard nothing. *They are at it. The new Godheads. Headcases. I told you, didn't I? The artillery.*

I heard it as Lanny passed my milk and ham sandwich over the counter. Not artillery, but the distinctive discharge of machine guns and high-powered rifles. The father gave me what almost amounted to formal lectures in weaponry as we listened on still evenings to the gun battles raging around the city. His verbiage was delivered, like an artillery barrage of the trenches in World War One, pounding me with words and exploding spittle, until I was ready to offer my unconditional surrender on the grounds of hygiene. I had to take into account that he was proud of his days in the old Official IRA, where he had handled a weapon or two, so a certain amount of attention from me was his due. *I wouldn't give these new lads the time of day,* he said dismissively of the new Republican movement, both the organisation, the direction and speed of their action. *They are all empty skites the lot of them.* He wasn't alone in this cynical view, but the new generation accused the old of cowardice and of being all talk.

Don't let them settle their eyes on you, young McGladdery, said Lanny in a surprisingly caring tone. *They are a wicked and criminal sort, the likes you've never met before,* said old, bent Lanny as I left the canteen. *This is God losing his way, these characters are Satan having his say.*

I recalled to mind his idea that an atheist is an unfearing person.

7.

Trust and obey, there's no other way to be happy in Jesus, I murmured. When I reached the bottom of the stairs on my way back to the chain—thinking that I should be unfearing of the chain as Lanny is of God—I could see that a collection of concerned gentry had gathered just outside the time office and close to the main gates, probably about fifty yards from where I stood. The aristocracy of the place, McCoffrey, the general manager, and several others of high rank in casual weekend wear—their slacks and heavy Aran pullovers from the wilds of Ireland—were demonstrating a form of hysteria.

In the midst of the aristocracy, O'Dunning the night security man was trying to stem the tide of panic. McCoffrey's hands chopped the air, then finger pointed here, there and everywhere as the gunfire outside mounted in intensity. O'Dunning's hands remained undemonstrative, one holding a fag low to his side, the other comfortably in his trouser pocket, but there was power in those hands of his, for the truth was, O'Dunning himself was a Provo. So the father insisted. Couldn't be, we said, he's the security man. The best man to have now, he said.

From my perspective the antics near the time office resembled a silent film. All extended gestures except for O'Dunning.

O'Dunning had some words for me one day, delivered to me without a gesture when I felt new and alone and weak on the chain. *If you've any problems here, son, just bring yourself and your problem to me*, he said. He sounded like Jesus, *Come unto me all ye that labour and are heavy laden and I will give ye rest.* Plenty of people labouring in here. I laboured. *He's no empty skite*, the father said of O'Dunning. He was the only Provo he would give the time of day to. People were not slow in giving the father the time of day even though the mother didn't and moved with ever increasing velocity to call him an empty skite.

I moved from the bottom of the stairs across the yard, my gaze still tilting towards the gate. The gunfire continued in intensity coming now from much closer to the bakery. In the streets directly outside, front and back. Those wee streets with hardly a space to turn around, with hardly a place to hide and take cover, except in the shadows.

I was probably a minute or two late getting back to relieve Malachi, so I broke into a jog. I moved swiftly on through the empty checking yard to the belt room still hearing a decent measure of the widely dispersed gunfire coming from all sides. I anticipated Malachi's anger which would manifest itself in an insane stare the moment I entered the beltroom and headed towards the chain.

Where the hell have you been? shouted Malachi in a wild falsetto whine. His gurning face told me he's fucked. He pulled a tray off the chain and slid it into the grooves on the half full bogie behind him and so was unable keep his angry gaze on me. Sweat was dripping off his forehead. He wheezed. I tried to grab the wire he had just pulled off the chain, gently, in order to make it appear that I wasn't exactly coming to his aid.

Don't touch it! Don't touch it you traitor! I used to be on the chain all the time you know, before you in fact. I know the chain. I know it more than you. And I don't know you at all. All I know is that you are the son of a traitor. When I'm on the chain there's no problem. I can handle the chain. You get in here because of your traitor Da. Turncoats and traitors you all are.

I allowed him to call the father a traitor. I allowed him to call me a traitor. I allowed him to talk freely and to think in the absence of protestations. I had an overwhelming urge to hit him. I should have hit him with words. And then booted him up the arse.

What the fuck are you doing Sloane, you fucking Fenian shite? said Jimmy Éclair coming out of nowhere. *Are your ears full of Fenian shite? Move. Get on those fucking bogies. Let McGladdery do his fucking job here.*

I took over the chain from Malachi who was now firmly in residence in my mind. I felt the warm steel on my palms once again and the coldness from Malachi's back as he walked away into the yards. He was to be a feared fly boy, fucked up and bitter and he had bad words for me. What fucked him up? His wife and kids and no permanent job at nineteen years old? Is that what suspended his smile? No, said everyone, Malachi never smiled since the day of his birth. It was conveyed to me that he was the Buster Keaton of the bakery. *But don't rely on him in a fight,* someone said. *And watch your arse side,* someone else said. Malachi's joylessness, all the maladies of his mind made him dangerous. He was the raw material for the discontented, for the cause. I feared his predictability, therein resided the possibility of a mad and unpredictable motive.

Malachi left me on the chain and disappeared through the dark entrance under the clock—now saying about seven fifty-eight p.m.—and into the cold checking yard where he continued in his task of searching for empty bogies.

I didn't see Malachi again in the bakery that night. Nearly two hours of the twelve-hour shift had shifted slowly. Slow time. The wait. Duration. The word itself is heavy. Heavier than time. Time is a fact, unreal. Duration is unthinkable as unreal, it has the weight of a granite gravestone. Oppressive. It's heavy on your mind. Made you feel sleepy. Not seeing, not knowing, not having. In history there were slow durations just as heavy. Christ in the

Garden of Gethsemane taunted by the devil for one. He desired the Lord's doubt. Had Jesus been able to rest it would have gone quicker but the devil never let him rest for a second. No time here in the garden. The garden, a symbol of life and growth became stagnant with evil. Satan said to Christ that his work will not be done. He will fail. But no, Christ said, I will master it as I will master you. Was it Malachi or McGraw who was the devil among the Irish legion?

Charge-hand Jimmy Éclair came alongside me to confide. He told me the bake will probably be finished at about two a.m. so it might be an early night for us all, if everything goes to plan. This was good news, spirit-lifting. I would then be skipping off home, so happy in the ghostly streets, not so scared of legless coalmen. Happy amongst the shooting empty skites. Who cares about that? That's nothing at all. Just go. Just run. Just laugh as you run. Beat the gun. Like in the war. Like a marine on D-Day. Head down, head for cover, into the covers of my bed and sleep. I looked back at the clock which was now reading only eight p.m.

I decided to concentrate on the job, attend to the movements. Thinking of the body and its repetitive actions I would soon be in a delightful inner dander.

I thought of the mind and body of the teenage half-wit Stanley Liptrot who craved attention from me and my friends. We played with his name and nominated him Stanley Lipwit or Stanley Trotlip, then Stanley Halftrot but finally, after monumental laughter, settled on Stanley Twitwit. He gave us many a laugh at his own expense, on account of his expense being mightily expansive.

One day he sauntered into our entry with his loose backward gait and seeing us sitting on and around a pile of builder's rubble came and stood before us unannounced, unwittingly being the entertainer. We studied him like lazy loutish naturalists for a new area of amusement. It wasn't a huge amount of duration before

Dominic the wise claimed that he was Elvis Presley. Stanley was not convinced at all initially, until he was emptied of all his doubt by Dominic's mimicking. He used his pen, taken from inside his school blazer, as a microphone and sung parts of *Blue Suede Shoes*. Dominic then asked Stanley if he wanted his autograph and when the answer came back as affirmative Dominic wrote on his forehead the word idiot.

Stanley walked off proudly saying he was going to show his mother. But when he reached the top of the entry he stopped, looked back and then shouted, *My name isn't Stanley anyway, it's Brett. Brett Maverick. And yous are liars! And yous are uncouth!* Then he charged us screaming like a loony lancer in the charge of the light brigade with his arm pointed out rigidly at Dominic. *Elvis liar bastard! Elvis bastard liar! Liar, liar, liar,* he cried as he flew past us, exiting the other end of the entry. We soon learned to be cautious of Stanley's form of madness.

Re-engaging with the job I thought to myself that I was the half-wit in this place.

What's this? says Alan, holding a book aloft. He had disappeared for a while and returned to me in the yard to hear the rest of what I had to say.

Serious words, I reply. *But there's humour in those serious words.* I thought of the words of Solomon the wise; *Even in laughter the heart is sorrowful, and the end of that mirth is heaviness.*

I hear Spinoza should have been arrested for substance abuse.

That's substantially serious Spinoza. He talked a lot about happiness and pleasure. But not a lot about laughing. Not many philosophers did. They didn't say what they found funny.

Some ventured a little to say what made things funny. With Hobbes it was all about superiority. I could never picture the great

Portuguese Jew, whose dark and sombre image I had in mind from a particular unnamed Rembrandt painting, rolling around in fits of uncontrollable laughter, holding his belly and begging for mercy. He looked a picture of total despair, not entirely in tune with his own philosophical recommendations. But, considering the lonely existence, his inherent weak health, his savage Jewish excommunication, cursed and cut off from society and friends, no wonder there was little humour in the man.

To the venerable blind Jorge in *The Name of the Rose*, laughing was a sin. By that he meant it was dangerous to the faith, to the hierarchy, to the institution. It is unsafe criticism. The special productivity of the small child, in the flow of learning a language, is something to take note of. Nothing is to hinder humour. The cross-eyed man, the hunchback, the dwarf, the blind Jorge himself with his rolling white marbles of eye balls, are all shown no pity by the inventive but immature mind. The grotesque physical appearance, the departure from the norm, is given special status, but also attests to a child's experience of perfection and beauty. The child soon finds that language is a power well worth a special effort. The adult sees that and seeks to hinder this effort and soon this well of inspiration dries up as the grown up sobers up.

8.

The almighty batch chain came to a grinding halt and created an immediate uncertainty. For a duration the individual racks swung and squeaked in their own fading momentum. Nothing now moved in the place where movement was everything The velocity that defined the way of effort was violated. Each man at his post adopted a pose of puzzlement. It was wonderfully silent and everyone stood in the silence of their very own wonder. In my arms I held a full batch tray and, with an unnerving wealth of time, slipped it smoothly into the bogie rails behind me and then stood as still as everyone else.

It occurred to me that the production for the night had finished. Had I been in my little trance for so long? A glance back at the clock told me that that was just a crazy notion. It was only eight forty-five. I glanced to my left taking in Éclair's office. He was absent, not in view. His papers fluttered on their hooks and pins in a breeze caused by a singular filthy little rotating fan on the office wall. Through the short tunnel to the yard beyond, in the darkness sitting behind the weak light, I heard forced whispering and the urgent scratching of shoe soles. Like someone being dragged about, and resisting the pull. The momentum now was towards listening. It was a time of inner and outer assessment.

Unexplained events cultivated the fear, so immediate explanations were called for. The expectation was that the belts might start up again as quickly as they stopped so everyone stayed put in case of that eventuality. Someone provided a tentative and extravagant explanation, to wit, that the electrical circuit, regulating the belts, had blown. It came from a confident proposer. That restored a little composure and the universal rigidity changed accordingly, to more relaxed postures, the phenomenon of undirected effort.

My attention was soon directed at McGraw. I could see he was resting his forearms on a bogie of pan bread that he had just packed. The men on the two-pound belt, Piggott and Pollock, stood together with arms folded and occasionally offered each other a whispered word. Big Man Meadow, from the belt right in front of me, juggled expertly with a couple of Veda fruit loaves and tried, at the same time, to hijack my attention to the delight of this piece of light entertainment. Then approaching footsteps in the tunnel. Éclair came out of its darkness from the packing room and, standing directly under the clock, told us to stay just exactly where we were. He hesitated as he encountered our general bewilderment. He moved over to where I was.

Dodos! Wildebeests, Oscar fucking wilde-fucking-beests, he muttered to me.

What the fuck's happening, Jimmy. It isn't the belt circuit, is it? shouted the Big Man Meadow.

Oscar fucking Wildebeests! spouted Éclair. *Dreamers in the moonlight. What fucking belt circuit? Circuit crap! I'll tell you when I fucking know, now I just know shite all. Shite all like you know. And all you know is shite. I know shite all and all you know is all shite. So, on this occasion, you know just as much as me. Fucking belt circuit! Your fucking head's missing a complete circuit, Meadow. Meadow by name, meadow in the head for your brain is a meadow, a fallow field full of empty shite. Shite doesn't move or think and that is what I want you all to do. Stay put like a lump of shite.* With this characteristic bombardment of insults he looked around in expectation of universal laughter, but only universal silence came his way. No one liked it. But it *was* funny. I almost laughed in Meadow's face. But he laughed in mine instead. I just smiled. Then he looked around and juggled happily with his loaves.

Yea Jimmy, but we don't want to be here all fucking night now, said Meadow, turning again to Eclair. He appealed for general support with open handedness, with a Veda loaf in each open claw. A universal hum of agreement was absent. Éclair stared at Meadow with his contemptuous charge-hand stare. It was almost unbearable.

You're on the fucking night shift, meadow brain. Night shift! You're supposed to be here all fucking night! Not wearing a shift at night in your empty bed, right, empty shite? Éclair disappeared back into the packing room, past the dim light that led to darkness.

My attention backtracked momentarily to what I saw when I was coming back from the canteen. The animated gentry at the gate, is that where Éclair was headed? But that line of thought was cut unceremoniously short when I saw the man McGraw shuffling my way. He was soon with me at close quarters. What nature would he make manifest?

The man McGraw was an utterly baffling character. A contradiction. A riddle even to himself. His modal engagement to the world, I assumed, was one of generally good affects. His relations to everyone at work seemed beneficial. What was he, however, in his own simple relation? How did he move from there to relations with others? At what rate? With what means? What fictions?

His initial form of friendship with me was grounded on a fiction, on the doubtful claim that it was knowledge he was after. He urged me time and again to enlighten him about the reformed faith of mine, and I fed it to him each time like a big fried breakfast. He couldn't get enough of it and was licking his slug-like lips for more. More, more, more, and I gave him more until I had difficulty thinking of more to give. Such was the magnitude of his interest at one point, I thought he desired to ditch popery and fully embrace the faith of Calvin and Luther. As I fell under the spell of his fiction, I thought I could lead him to Christ, to have him bow before the saviour and repent, but he only wanted to embrace me, and lead me to bow before him.

In my excitement to tell him of predestination, limited atonement, total inability and irresistible grace I didn't see that he simply wanted my excitement. My diamond lively eyes he saw in other settings. His perpetual questioning was simply a means to get my lips moving. When I talked he studied my mouth and left his own open wide as though my words were entering directly into that orifice. He knew intuitively that a thing is what it does, there is no being at an instant.

If everything I do is an instance of God's will and not an instance of my own will, then it is all OK? Isn't it? Everything is permitted? he said when he perused predestination. All the old hat! *Nothing to feel guilty about. Do you ever feel guilty?*

Yes, I do. Sometimes. But it is not a matter of guilt.

What do you feel guilty about? Is it in your head? An underneath thought? Unconscious.

I don't know, but the important thing is to follow your nature, that your actions are yours.

And do you follow your nature?

It is hard to say. Everything is so fragmented, I am still only seventeen. Striving to follow your nature is the thing. But we only ever think in part. For we know in part and we prophesy in part, but when that which is perfect is come then that which is in part shall be done away, said St Paul.

Striving, yes, striving. And I like the idea of being a part, a fragment of the whole. It means, God means, that we should come together and love each other. That immediately sounded wrong to me, and increasingly mistaken the more I thought it was him who said it.

I don't know because some things are bad and bad to combine with. Like the Devil.

So now, in the still belt room, the slippery serpent wanted my movement.

Listen. There's something wrong, something serious going on, he whispered in my ear. *I think we should go out there in the yard and have a look. Just you and me, now. If something's going on we don't want to be fucking about here. Know what I mean?*

I don't know if I do get you. What do you think it is? Is it safe out there if something is going on? Y'know Éclair told us to stay put here? Probably in case the belts start up. Here's the best place to be.

Fucking Éclair. Let me tell you about Éclair. He wouldn't give a fuck about us here even if there was a fuck to give, but he doesn't because he only gives a fuck about number one. If something's going on out there Éclair'll be interested in his own arse alone. He'd be out in the fresh air. Fresh air Éclair he'd be. At least we might know something and knowing makes it safer. Knowing nothing makes it dangerous. Knowing something means we could then judge what to do for ourselves. Self-preservation. That's what it's all about. Is self-preservation anywhere in all those ideas of yours?

The manner of his little speech made me nervy and uncertain, expressed, as it was, with a tight-lipped dramatic urgency, quietly in a place where there was no need for such caution. I could imagine the mad scramble to get on the side of safety. He was right about knowing, about knowing what was happening, having something in our heads to be able to make a judgement. Éclair was right all right, we all knew shite. We were all empty skites, skittering about in the dark. Ignorance was not helping the nerves. All sorts of devils were on the loose out there. What did old Lanny say? He knew something. We should know what was really going on.

Know what the gentry at the gates knew. The gates were closed, that's right, the gates were never closed. We just had to be careful that's all, I told McGraw.

Look, Seamus, son, at the very least we can just take a wee peep. You're a wise lad. Use your wisdom. Just take it easy, step by step, see if we can at least see something. There could be a bomb in the place. Some nut headcase could have put one in here anywhere. Everyone is somewhere else. A Prod, a Fenian wanting it to look like a prod. Ticking, ticking, ticking away, ticking our lives away while we stay put here waiting for lousy fucking loaves. Do you want to be blown to hell for a loaf? Ending up in hell clutching a fucking loaf wrapper? Ticking down to a big bread explosion. Remember what happened at the bus station round the corner? Arms and legs in all the directions of the route map on the bus station wall! When those passengers arrived at that station I bet they didn't consider getting a free ride on a bus going all the way to eternity. If Éclair went out to find out what was going on and he was told it was a bomb scare do you think he would come the whole cut back here and tell us? Maybe he would, maybe he wouldn't. But my guess is he would get offside and scram especially if it's twenty or twenty-one bombs like on Bloody Friday. No reflection on you but he's a prod too and he's not going to risk his prod neck for a bunch of thick micks like us in here. What do you think, Seamus?

Out of the belt room we went, through the unlit tunnel I followed McGraw's shuffle. We stood there in the huge spaces of the packing room, reduced by the emptiness to minimum momentum to move in any particular direction. Anxiously we stared around us, strained staring to distant corners. Stacked from one end of the room to the other were rows and rows of bogies full of bread and buns ready to be loaded on to lorries to be taken the length and breadth of the province, to all those rosy-cheeked country faces who couldn't live without their buns and bread. Every day for them was a breaking of bread day. A holy day. But the gates were closed. They were never closed! They had to be open.

To the right of us, a little further on, was the entrance to the fancy pastry room with all the deluxe sweet cakes and creams. It's where the women worked by day, but never at night. What worked at night in their absence was the frustrated imagination. Beyond the pastry room, further up to the right again, was the lorry loading bay where the huge articulated lorries roared in and out through the main gates. Further beyond that were the fridge-like wide open wastes and unlit corners of the yards that were not used for anything in particular. Even on summer days you could see your breath down there. In the farthest corner ahead of us, as far as you could go, to the left side as you walked from the main belt rooms, was a small wooden gate, which led directly to the narrow back streets behind the bakery. It was unused and always padlocked.

At this point I felt alone in the man McGraw's universe of desire. I saw clearly his intentions. He would slip me into one of the cold, dark corners and start his groping and touching like never before, and without fear of interference he would encounter the tender places that his fingers had never before visited. He would break into his own soliloquy of soul and body seduction, his exceptionally wild will would be set free. I would be helpless. Before that I tried to insert into his thoughts my final procrastinatory ideas of reservation, which were now leaping out of my mouth in disturbed desperation.

I'm just not so sure what to do. I'm doubting—I mean I'm not sure what is wise here. We have to be wise. This could be very serious. You say I'm wise, but I am not sure, but surely the wise thing to do now is to go back. We may be walking right into something, into somebody else's plans, and the belts might just start up again back there. Maybe just one of us should go and the other go back there to check. Maybe I should toddle back there. Éclair's probably back there with some news and looking for us.

With a deep breath of impatience, he turned himself away from me and walked a little further into the packing room and away from the belt room. He stopped after a few steps and then beckoned me to come, first with his dirty, crooked finger and then with his head. He had his own plans.

We'll just take a wee dander and have a gander, like I said, and that's all. Not go beyond that. And we should stick together, you know how in films they always split up and you know they shouldn't. If the belts start up, well fucking what about it? It's only bread for God's sake. I felt compelled to move at his pace and in his direction. There was a sudden potency in his tone. The few steps he took to open up a space between us, had a magical affect, the distance directly proportional to the power of his will. The magical will to arouse me to participate in his ends. The end in part being an initiation. He saw the weakness and took me by the arm.

Now come on. Let's go. Don't you worry. You'll be safe with me. You don't want to be buried under a load of loaves and shite if the place goes up. Do you? You want to see the morning. Another day. Come on. You will be with me, in my care. Safe.

McGraw, easing forward in his laceless, loose shoes, felt my resistance and knew it to be weak. Having established his control with his grip, he let my arm go and walked slowly ahead. I was dragged in his wake by the stronger force that was his way over mine.

I re-acquainted myself with the deserted nature of the place. The coldness of the place. A coldness that, when it gets to your bones, makes the body shrink. No grinding, no squeaks, no clanging, no echoing voices, nothing. Just the noise inside your ears. A humhiss. What we should have seen here were the packers doing their jobs, with their stubby pencils and long paper slips in their hands, busily filling their orders on the bogies, but nothing was happening. After a few steps we stopped and stood at the door of the pastry room and looked in. Not a Will's Whiff of a worker. Not even the ghostly trail of sweat or perfume. Not a whiff or a swirl of a spirit.

Out of the ears went the silent humhiss and in came more gunshot cracks. Inside or outside we knew not. Sometimes close sometimes distant, and the further we proceeded through the yard the clearer and more discretely audible they became. We passed the lorry loading bay from where we could see the main gate. The agitated gentry had gone. One lorry waited in isolation, its back doors wide open and tail lift down, ready for its full cargo of empty bogies to be unloaded. Absent were bogie men and the lorry driver.

The main gate was visible down each side of the lorry. Still closed. The loudest cracks of gunfire came from that direction. We looked back and around and all over the place. With the main gate closed the feeling was that the whole bakery was sealed off with us sealed in. I looked to McGraw for some inspired decision.

It's a queer thing all right, isn't it? It's really queer. It's so close. Have you seen anything as queer as this before? I asked him, but there was no reply. He just looked at me like a dumb animal. I imagined the chain had started up again, I imagined I heard it, with the batch trays revolving endlessly with no one to remove them. The bakers above stamping up their legendary floury mist. McGraw settled his lusty lazy eyes on me.

Let's just have a look out of the wee back gate over there… and then we'll go back, back to the belts like you want. We'll belt it back to the belts if we see nothing. His way with words wasn't amusing. *I think I know what's going on. That's all I'm asking.*

He was lying, the sly fly child of Satan spoke his native language of lies.

But it's always shut that gate, shut and locked, there's no point. McGraw fed me an annoyed expression. The small back gate was beckoning and he no longer was in the mood for pleading. But sure enough there was now some activity beyond the small door.

Did you hear that? A shout. Come on. There's a crack in the door that you can see through to Raphael Street. Through the crack we will see the world. Like we know a woman through her crack. He smiled. The mention of a woman and a woman's crack lifted my mood. These were more magic words, this magic was a form of enslavement. It was the magic that was all over the place in words of all sorts. It was in rituals and rites, the magical motive was to capture minds, engage their weaker emotions, make minds think things that were not in their nature to think. Even made them do mad things like a drunk man does.

I felt a sudden intoxication, an arousal from the depths. McGraw would have more words for me. He had administered to me an extensive vocabulary of sin and evil. Words of wonder. Words that combined to make intoxicating notions. Notions that were potions of pleasure. Ideas that felt at home and charmed the doubting mind into doubting its doubt. He talked of firmness and softness, the dizziness of closeness, wetness and warmth, touched textures of smoothness and tinglings of all manner, the tightness and looseness, the sweet smells, the noises of desperate delight, the shape of things, the movement of shapes, that would have me hovering in over abyss of ecstasy. Nothing of this was new, there was a strong sense of recollection, in the Platonic sense, the effort of the universal already within, the apriori which McGraw depended upon to move ahead with his strategy.

I have moments of complete madness, I blurted out, *moments that have me bursting in desperate need. I perspire and pant and swear as if they were natural words. I sometimes cry.*

That's your manhood talking, he said. *All natural and proper. You just need to let it flow out. Don't restrain it. If you allow me I will lead you.*

Alan the Listener broke in and broke his long silence. *Did you follow?*

I did follow, but not him, I followed the body. My body.

But your body followed? So you followed.

I followed the man McGraw to that little back gate with the small slit in it through which we could see the world outside. I wished for him to tell me with certainty that he would arrange an encounter with the wetness and dizziness and the tinglings and everything else he described, and to make it that very night. I was prepared to lower my resistance to him in the meantime in the hope of that event being realised quickly. So I expressed the wish to him—about the women he mentioned from time to time—and he promised it without hesitation. He smiled with a delight of his own.

Through the thin vertical crack in the gate we peered. I could see very little immediately through the powerful blackness. Then the universals went to work. Crude at first, shapes, textures, movements. My powers of imagination went to work mentally adjusting, supplementing and correcting the menagerie of the boundlessly unformed. The unformed became bodies uniformed, the shiny objects on black were buttons. Beautiful B-Special buttons for brutes to fasten an elegant tunic. Elegance and brutality in one form.

What was then given was like a theatrical event. Partly a pantomime performance indeed. Slapstick. Slipping. Skids and shuffles from the soles of shoes on those shiny wet cobbles.

Rhythmic up and down motions of the unidentified uniforms accompanied by loud grunts, yelps, barks, forced out of a shape by considerable physical effort. Soon the pantomime stage became a torture chamber. Squeals of souls in pain, pleading tones in voices, firm controlled utterances, orders, panicked shouts that echoed up the dark street and back through the crack into our ears, thuds of soft bodies against hard objects, the groans of the tormented with injured bodies. McGraw bent and looked more closely through the vertical crack. He moaned as if he was with the tortured souls in their moments of anguish.

Poor fuckers! whispered McGraw. *Those poor brave fuckers. They're in for it now. They're in a soapy bubble all right. The peelers have them well and truly by the republican ideals. Trapped they are. Here. What do you think Seamus?* He backed away, stood up and stretched his back, leaving me alone to look. My eye blinked as the icy flow of air entered the crack and a cold tear fell down my cheek.

Laughing continued in between the shouting, with howling and heavy breathing in fine accompaniment. New words of pleading emanated from a wispy grey obscured shape on the ground. It was picked up and thrown back down on to the cobbles to be kicked by shiny black boots. Voices from beyond the scope of my roving eye on the draughty crack, shouted.

If he wants a fight give him one. Go on! Give him it. Go on Jimmy ye boy, kick his head in, fuck the Fenian freedom fighter! Give him a wee glimpse of Fenian heaven. Show him what freedom is. Give him a fucking idea of the freedom of the jack boot. That's it, Jimmy, go on ya boy!

As I anticipated some further horror to come and ruminated on its possible form, I felt McGraw adjusting himself to my rear. He applied himself to a sneaky seduction. His usual approach was from behind in order not to see any sign of resistance in my eyes. From there he whispered in my ear.

Satin bows descending on suspended elastics. Sitting pretty on silk stockings. Silk stocking on pale, glassy smooth legs. A whore with a cock lies with legs wide open. Joy. Lips rooted in nature as beautiful buds. Where a bud is at home without turning into a flower. But that cannot happen. A bud always transforms into a leaf or a flower or it dies undeveloped or becomes another thing. The bud must be appreciated in its time. Its home is here and now.

Is that what he said?

That's what I heard.

That's not at all his language, said the Listener.

The torture continued beyond the small door. I still had my eye at the crack. A naked upper body is fondled by foreign hands that spread to every sensitive part, pressing, caressing the lean and limp living cold flesh. Firm hands stripped the torso clean to give it special treatment.

McGraw was arriving at his desired destination behind. My eyes remained open to what was before me by way of torture. The moaning from behind and before presented to my ear an appropriate harmony, as did the breeze upon my eye and the hot breath on my neck.

What do you find? McGraw whispered. *Good or bad? Or painful?* He breathed heavily after his words.

Excessive, I say. *Shocking.*

Did you find anything else?

I was caught cold. The McGraw touch was still to be felt. The pleasure of it was undeniable but I couldn't see how that was possible as the source of it was so unpleasant, ugly, and in every respect threatening. And if there was pleasure it didn't entail joy.

Come back with me, will you? he asked. *Away with me.* His normal breathing pattern was resuming but his tone was drunk with desperation. He slurred. He dribbled. His head fell back and wobbled on an unsure neck. *Joy is just round the corner. Hardly any distance at all. And we'd be safe. Lovely and safe. Nothing to fear. No more nuisance.*

I wailed inside for Jesus. I moaned audibly for the devil. I damned the fat skitter now before me for the deep hell hole I was in. What I wanted was to be at home, to be at peace. Somewhere. But not all of me. McGraw wanted his home as well. He wanted to extend his home to accommodate me. I stalled. In between the two worlds I looked for a compromise, something that will say neither yes or no, that will not deny him totally or declare a complete affirmation.

What does he offer? asks Alan the Listener.

He offers me Joy Street. A suitable situation, I reply. *A remedy for the body. A direction, a focus for the mind which perceives too many things at once.*

Does he offer you another body?

Indeed so. And it was all so present to me and I wanted nothing to cut it off. I banished Christ so that he would not interrupt it. He offered it that very night. He offered the female presence, their bodies, the ones he ranted on about before to tease me to hell. So I told him, as I had before, that if only he could get the women there, I'd go with him.

My body had been modified by his words about the women and I wanted it modified by the actual presence of their bodies. I desperately wanted that contact to happen, to have a soft feminine hand grasp me where McGraw had, and finish off what he had started. McGraw was merely a substitute for the women.

I know what you're thinking, he said. *Don't worry, if you are going to come I can get them to come. You think that's a problem, don't you? It's no problem at all. Easy to arrange, I know them you see. So come, come.* His confidence was startling. It was said so softly and enticingly and he repeated the words: *come, come, come.* Over and over again he repeated the word whilst laying out his open hands before me in a suggestion of what was easily within his power.

Are you sure, I spluttered with joy. *Are you absolutely sure? Do you promise?* He nodded his promise and I believed him. I saw us there with two women, without definite identity, but with all their feminine willingness to see to and enjoy my eager young unpolluted, extended being. I saw laughing faces and heard joyous noises. The overpowering ideas of the body would be given their true and proper expression in McGraw's house that night.

I didn't want any further confirmation, I simply wanted him to talk more about what I had already accepted. I wanted information about who they were and what they looked like, about their willingness and inhibitions.

I don't mean later, I mean now! Right now. We'll fuck off now. Just think of a beautiful crack of a cunt for your cock to sink into, he said moving a pace forward and sliding his hand between my legs. *This is a night you'll never forget. The night you'll smell a woman for the first time, and that'll calm that madness in you. I promise there will be at least one wee whore there. The boy will be the man after tonight. A man. A real Belfast man. A man with full set of balls with an empty ball sack. And do it right and there'll be no end to your pleasure. They'll rub their long fingers through that long black hair of yours and you'll feel their pointed polished nails on your skull. You'll explode in your head. You'll still be erupting up the road as you're going home. You'll never feel the same. Your body will be yours. You'll know it at last.*

He came closer and applied some enthusiastic upward pressure with his hand just at the moment he said *pleasure* and then withdrew it as if to withdraw the pleasure. As I felt it, it was not his hand at all, it was a foretaste of what was in store if I went with him. The saviour Jesus Christ had apparently no power in this area, in the place of quivering tongues, babblings and writhings.

Nothing shall be able to separate us from the love of God, said St Paul. Here that seemed untrue. Another spirit rushed in to claim the void. I felt the heat of hell roasting me to a turn. A fine platter awaited the man McGraw.

Would I ever find the inseparable love of God again?

9.

That's the conscience, said the wily Pentecostal preacher, in every sermon. He meant the moral consciousness, the idea in the mind that duplicates itself in order to judge itself. The most real of ideas, of the highest worth, he said. He was ultimately a man of fact, and the divine act, out of nowhere, became a divine fact. He knew that in order to experience something as an act of God he must first know what an act of God was. In relying on consciousness to access truth, however, he and his followers took effects for causes and so were condemned to a seriously flawed understanding. But they were not mad, or even on the road to madness, as some thought, when they heard them on the streets proclaiming the Gospel. Mad people do not reflect upon their own lunacy.

I followed the flawed understanding and desired desperately to know what an act of God was in their fashion? There was something in the behaviour itself that was desirable. But one minute I thought I had the anointing, the next I knew I hadn't, then I had it again. If you already had it, why was it such a slippery thing? The preacher said if you think in a doubting way then you haven't got it, you have the Devil instead, pretending to be God.

At a certain point church was everything. What was the church? It was no cold cathedral. It was a warm welcoming place. It was a fiery furnace of active faith. When firmly within the church, the world was the lie. *Wherever the crowd is, is untruth.* Rarely were any other words apart from holy scripture quoted, but this message from Kierkegaard found favour. As did that of the Stoic: *Retire into yourself as much as you can. For you must inevitably hate or imitate the world.*

Are you following the way of truth and not the way of the world? the pastor said. Taking me to one side, he aligned himself with me, in that latitudinal way of his, setting himself square. With his healing hands on my shoulders he would apply his powerful gift of discernment, looking inside me to divine the authentic spirit of joy. *Come with me and we'll pray together.* In a small prayer room, he set himself square again, with me kneeling under his full spiritual and corporeal uprightness. He laid his powerful healing hands on my head and prayed for my God joy to return and for my sad attention to the Devil and his ways to depart. Had he caught that wandering eye when it should have been closed in prayer? Wandering over the bowed heads to find a fancy. Seeing a female willing to return my friendly gaze in equally friendly measure. Had he, whilst preaching the four square Gospel, spotted me lounging in my seat looking for all I was worth like a slave to the carnal daydream? Nothing of this could be hidden, nor could it be made consistent with the life of a saint.

McGraw was a wild, desperate man. *You're simply so cute,* he said. This odd compliment was far too sweet and delicate an expression to have been formulated in his clumsy capacity for thought. He had nothing of the poet in him. Did I hear him or was it the woman he promised?

Fresh fruit cute, ready for picking. Fruition of his desire. For him I was as close to a pretty female as he could hope for. I was lean and flat, hairless and all woman to him, even though cuntless. He imagined me in all his private ways, transforming me into the womanly thing.

I see the woman! he declared. There was laughter in me suddenly but McGraw's wrath was something to fear. He stroked the upright naked shape slowly, minimally and murmured something indecipherable that I took to be an expression of satisfaction. Occasionally he stopped moving entirely this or that part of his body to reacquaint himself with the source of his joy and dispel unwanted ideas of distraction. What artificiality did he endow me with? What did he make of me? What class was I an instance of for him, over and above the natural boy with plump lips, the thick hair, and the smooth, tight body? Not the static image, a picture he would preserve for my absence. *When you have found the light within yourselves, you will know as you are known. Affectio* and *affectus* would cover it.

On his bended knees he performed an act of devotion, exclaimed with a distinguished depravity, his excitement fast flowing from that centre of ferment and then through his whole body to his erupting mouth. The talent of tongues descended upon him. Out of the sea of babbling he hissed a series of Seamuses before embarking on an effortless mantra. *Seamus, Seamus, Seamus. Mercy on me. Pity me. Pure provider. Oh you cutie cunt pie, look at you, little girlie boy. Perfect joy. Blessed be this joy. Love me. I feel the goodness in me that you are.* He passed on to perform a little song expressed with an ecstatic laugh. *This little cock of mine, I'm going to let it shine. This little cock of mine...* a semi-religious ditty, the other half, pure, old music hall. Then back to the warbling expression of mad inner thoughts. *Oh give me your pure little hole... Give me your cutie pie hole for my throbbing thing. Take me to heaven. Heaven, I'm in heaven...* The words emerged with great gusts of asthmatic breath and great strings of yellow saliva.

I had a tune in my own head. *I need thee, oh I need thee, every hour I need thee, oh bless me now, my saviour, I come to thee.* But it was a powerless prayer. God wasn't there. I stayed where I was.

We were thus oddly together in one of the dimly lit tunnels when the whole building seemed to be on the point of collapse. The enormity of the sound that came rushing towards us snatched our otherwise engaged minds. McGraw's act of concentrated devotion on his knees before me was painfully abandoned as he ducked like a cowardly cunt in a calculated act to save his head from being sliced off. There was no movement within sight and no apparent cause. The man McGraw had the suffering look in his eye.

It came from somewhere near the gates, I suggested, more to avert McGraw's wanton attention and pin it to the imminent peril. The ear-splitting noise dropped away and ushered in a new silence. The violence from outside the broken back gate, now at our backs, had subsided too. McGraw stood up, I wrestled with my whites and we moved slowly to the junction of the yard and the lorry bay, from where we could once again see the front gates. The articulated lorry was still there as before, parked with its tail gate down, still with a cargo of empty bogies. Several bogies had, however, fallen out and were lying at angles partly attached to the tail gate, and partly on the ground. That accounted for the noise, but not the cause of it.

10.

How the Sunday morning communion service confounded the sinful soul and inspired the erotic schism, the sensual split. Sharpening the wit and widening the clit. What if no one here is worshipping God? It came in a flash and I started babbling like a baby. Like a Jacky B baby. Simultaneously I was interpreting my very own words. Drink ye all of it, ye all from timeless cup. Romance the pouting lips, treat the trembling tongue. Substantial adulterated mingling in salivating cavity confined. Crucified cocktail in emptied heads, swooning swirling gathering unrefined. Spinning out the spiritual energy, shaking out the inner demon. In sweaty budding beads, sucking in the breath of God. This union of quivering saints. Heads and hands heaven bound, unbound dancing body giving forth life entire to unseen ground.

I truly love the schismatics, announces Alan. *Inspired by the Devil himself was it? The schismatics of love.*

The pastor of the church unwittingly. He was the only one of his kind. I told him. *Do you understand? He was a sorcerer. And I saw it.*

I do understand. Even though you cannot have a kind of one. That would be contradictory. Identifiable individuality in difference. What do you think of that?

Well yes, you cannot have identity in sameness. In resemblance. The old Scholastic distinction of a distinction without any difference.

But go on then. Tell me about the church, will you? This is where there's sense in all you're telling me. Take me through a sermon. To find its source of sorcery.

You may be right. It's an invitation I cannot refuse. *It's where I make my way in moments of extreme anxiety. To consolidate the emotions. Where I fall under the spell.*

It'll take a degree of patience. But this is where the man is desperate to fully affirm God, but it is a failed affirmation as he makes God a failed being just like himself. His truth rests on an emotional and ethical foundation. The spell. His charm. It has an accidental power as well as an essential one.

That is what I see.

Pastor Davy Prebble had a powerful energy for the sermonizing business. He preached his guts out in a cramped upper room in an old Orange Hall in Protestant east of the city from the age of sixteen, until the guts gave in. His finitude was mostly in his guts. His church congregation itself was a marvellous miscellany of human finitude. Minds and bodies were drenched in contingency. It provided me with my first awareness of necessity. Elect and unelect came from all corners of the Ulster province to witness a masterly performance, in technique if not in content. He was not an educated man, the dogma was suspect, but the expression of sorcery was unparalleled.

This is what modern man is afraid of, so he institutes an act of terrorism against it. Intellectual lynch law. Defamation. The man of God is a scientific imbecile. What form of madness was in his performance? If the pastor had have been cutting his nails and destroying them in a private ceremony before coming to church, or tossing bones to the wind, I could not have rejoiced more in his spiritual integrity. But that was precisely what he was doing in the church itself. The event that was the church service was the whole magical rite and it stood as function apart form the dogma itself. Thus the sermon must be observed as a ceremony and not as an intellectual exercise to achieve certain forms of understanding. Nothing will happen without the rite for the rite is the magic itself.

So this is how it was on a particular occasion. The fact that I can relate it almost verbatim attests to the almost absurd way in which Prebble's words and actions wormed their way into my head and found a permanent home. But pay attention to the way of the words, the delivery, the approach, as much as the words themselves. This religious undertaking is quite unique, linking it to art and amusement, in that emotion aroused is discharged at the time of arousal, but unlike them, such is its power, it is carried on through into everyday life.

Some called the after-effects miracles, when the affects in daily life were good. The effects on illnesses most notable. The power was given, taken, firmly fortified and established, then re-distributed in the lives of suitable receivers. The pastor was called a *live-wire* for good reason. He was its source and driving energy.

He came late on purpose, the service having already started, to march up the aisle, singing and dancing and clapping on each side of him. Designed to instil a sense of invincibility. The church was in effect at war with the world, on a crusade. The first utterance in every sermon was always sensational.

Nicodemus! A rasping bellow blistered the hearing and tested hearing aids. The name Nicodemus entered my ear as the name James Mason for I always saw the holy James Mason as Nicodemus. Nicodemus Mason. *Nicodemus ...a rabbi, prominent member of the Jewish Council, searched his soul and considered that his social circumstances to be good enough to secure for him salvation.* Prebble stepped back from the pulpit and wandered in its full latitude, looking thoughtfully and intently at his people, with an expert performer's deliberation as to when and how he should issue his next dramatic words. Like a comedian setting up the punchline. Then the words came in a powerfully rhythmic barrage accompanied by the corresponding rhythms of the body. Every movement represented a step in the ceremonial dance. It was not, as he followed in his folly, a spirit descending upon him, moving his body for him.

Well brethren what of that thought? Good enough! Nicodemus thought it was good enough to be born into a Jewish family—he thought. It was good enough to be obedient to the law—he thought. It was good enough to be a member of the Jewish High Council—he thought. But friends... His voice is now a delicate whisper into the microphone. *Friends, it was not good enough.* Then an immense shout that lifted some tense bottoms off their seats: *I tell you now it was not!* Prebble's hands chopped down on the red, brushed velvet *JESUS SAVES* pulpit top. He then took a step back and paused. His body shook as his soul resonated within. With closed eyes he looked blindly heavenward. He raised his arms to heaven. The first signs of sweat appeared on his crisp, white shirt, in the armpits and chest and the upper back. He wiped his brow with a crisp, clean, folded handkerchief taken from his trouser pocket, returning it to the pocket still in folded form. He looked around and waited for the just-administered idea to filter through. He judged the moment to perfection. A buzz of enthusiasm was apparent and acted as a gauge of the general awareness. Under his gaze, the hum quickly turned into a ferment of joy. He afforded a smile in response before he walked back again to his pulpit in a terrifying seriousness. He karate chopped his open Bible as the words came again, each word chaperoned by a singular chop.

It was not good enough! He swept the hand horizontally. *Unless a man has been born over again he cannot see—cannot see to enter—the kingdom of God. Nicodemus, great spiritual leader though he was—a Pharisee, but a Pharisee who couldn't see beyond the end of his Jewish nose —was spiritually blind. He had his spiritual eyes poked out at birth by a blunt Jewish tradition. Blind! A blind man unable to see beyond his tradition, a respected religious figure unable to think of the spirit instead of the flesh. And so friend, what is it that Nicodemus asks? What is it that he asks? Now listen friend, listen closely. Look at me. Nicodemus asks; How is it possible for a man to be born again when he is old? Can he enter his mother's womb a second time and be born?*

Prebble scanned his congregation. He shook his head. He clasped his hands and placed his elbows on the top of the pulpit.

Oh poor Nicodemus. He laughed out these words and looked heavenward like he was laughing with God. *Intelligent all right. Oh yes, he had a great mind. The intelligent fool! Yes, the world is full of them. Full of fools. The kingdom of fooldom is full. Can you picture him brethren? Old Nic. A man of his social standing, of his intellectual ability, has his whole world swept from beneath him. All his certainties have become doubts and he stands where all men must stand at one point in their lives. In front of Almighty God, in front of the truth! I am the truth says Jesus. I am the way. The truth is God and God is the truth and it is where we all end up at some point or other. The truth. It is not different for each age, it does not vary with time or social setting. It is as it is. In the beginning was the word and the word was with God and the word was God. The word is the truth. God is the word, the word his breath of life, God is truth. The truth of true life. The life of the true word. And despite all that we read and learn in the scriptures we still wantonly throw our souls to the wind. We live for anything that the mind conceives in its weakest moments, and blind ourselves to the truth. We live for personal glory but this is to be the life of the living dead. We live but are spiritually dead. We uproot ourselves from the source of growth. We perish for the wisps of pleasure, for the passing satisfaction. Paul says,—But God forbid that I should glory, save in the cross of our Lord Jesus Christ by whom the world is crucified unto me and I unto the world. God forbid that I should glory in my birth, my education, my proficiency in scripture or my regard for ritual. What things were gain to me, those I counted loss for Christ. If anything sums up the Gospel, that is it. And here we are at the crossroads of our society. The road of the cross is our crossroad. In the year nineteen and seventy two we are at war with our fellow citizens. Or are we? No friend, we are at war with the Devil, evil itself, the evil in the world, and so with the world. We are the modern day crusaders. The men of violence are the Devil and his demons incarnate, they are his army of evil. Instances of sin. They are his demons doing his work. They don't need arrested, or given justice, they need to be exorcised. But friends this is a blessing, yes, a blessing to us that we cannot ignore. We struggle with the ultimate power of evil in our own community. And we talk and walk without fear. Nothing shall separate us from the love of our God. Praise the Lord!*

But we are nevertheless in danger. We still glory in everything that is not only ultimately worthless, which is by itself made our ultimate end but which is ultimately the source of everything evil. Tradition, education, ritual in its own right. Money! Valueless things in themselves, the things of a valueless world. Listen to me friends. Hear these words, think these thoughts. Think of Nicodemus. How can a man be born again? he asks. How? How? How? He pleads. He strives day after day, seeking an answer. Ah, says the Lord, and here preacher Prebble took a step back from the pulpit, threw out his chest, squinted his eyes, raised his hands to heaven, preserved the significant silent moment, and then in a breathy breeze of a whisper delivered the words that penetrated every attending ear with precision. *The wind bloweth! The wind bloweth!* Then an aimed windy whisper all around one hundred and eighty degrees, *the wind bloweth, the wind bloweth.* He sucked in and blew out to imitate the wind and accompanied it with a little jig. *O--o-o-oh the wind bloweth!* he cried out to heaven. *The wind bloweth! The wind bloweth brethren. It bloweth mightily!* With these words inflicting a kind of temporary spiritual madness, a moment of apparent loss of control, he took flight off the raised platform and landed his heavy frame inches from the first row of worshippers. Up close they saw that greater extent of his madness, and so felt a greater extent of their own fear. He walked crab-like (an inebriated crab) along the row expressing his next words to the rigidly upright individuals in front of him. *Oh, you know the sound but don't know from whence it comes or to whither it goes. And so it is friends with everyone who is born of the spirit. Do not look to men, to a creed, even to a church, to a political power, to a school of thought. The wind bloweth! The wind bloweth! and it is here tonight in our very midst. Listen. Listen. Do you hear it? Do not fight it. Listen to it. Let it blow you towards Jesus. Listen, let Jesus inhale your soul. Listen to the wind.* He paused and put his hand to his ear to hear. A significant pause. A pregnant pause and *he* knew exactly what made a pregnant pause pregnant. The silence operated as spirit as it had done so many times before and as the preacher made his way back to the pulpit, the alarmed souls in his wake became charged by that spirit.

Back in the pulpit he breached his silence. *Open your soul up to it. It is power, it is life, it is peace, peace, real peace. Not the peace of this or that politician. Not this peace process or that peace process, but the peace within. The peace of mind. The peace of the soul. Peace of our spirit. Who is that talking to you? I know you can hear it. It's Jesus. It's Jesus. Softly and tenderly.*

I heard McGraw say softly and tenderly, *Come with me, you're weary, come home with me and be a man.* I was divided. To look or to listen. I listened. I chose the Pastor for the moment.

Christ died not for the good but the vilest creatures in his creation, the lowest in our communities. The beasts, the monsters, the murderers. Sin will no longer have a claim on you. You will never be separated from the love of God.

———

Murderers, monsters, beasts. That series of ideas was where I was in reality, brutally back to the cold yard far from the world of the word of God to the words of mammon McGraw. McGraw was close, closer than Jesus, something I didn't think was possible. He was his own inadequate bodily expression of a perfect, divine creation. I knew he had no idea in his head of this pure redeeming world. But I felt at that time there was such power in this world of the pure spirit, that anyone, even McGraw, coming into contact with it would be unable to resist it.

If only he could just be persuaded into the presence of the holy Preacher Davy Prebble, to feel the renewing reverberations of his mighty message, he would no longer make lust his governing aim of life. It would be inevitable. At this moment however, I felt trapped with no possibility of escape. I was in his world with his rules, the rules I was more and more willing to follow. He was converting me to his truth and convincing me of his way to salvation. The place was as quiet at this point as I had ever experienced it. Just standing there, still, in the still absence of spirit, in the cold physical world, I heard my own body creak with weakness.

Trapped! declared McGraw emphatically. *Do you feel trapped, Seamus?* The ambiguity of his question struck me immediately. Trapped by him or that we were both in the trap here not knowing what to do? He spoke before I answered. He spoke in a gritty whisper.

Here is a story of trappedness. I was playing an exhausting game with my big fat father—and he was big, huge—playing before bed, something like wrestling, but just messing about. It got rough. I got into bed exhausted and lay looking up at him breathing heavier and heavier as he came closer to me, as he usually did, to tuck me in and give me a rub on the hair and a kiss. But as he got closer he never stopped getting closer and his heavy breathing became a loud gasping. His body eclipsed the small light on the other side of the room and then the whole room itself as he dropped on top of me as dead as a dodo. A dead dodo weight. I felt this massive fucking weight on my chest and stomach and especially on my chest and I struggled to get from under him but couldn't shift the massive frame. My arms were locked beneath him and only a part of my head and my legs peeped out from under him. I could get no leverage to get him off or get from under him. I shouted at him to get off, not knowing entirely his state of deadness. Maybe, I was thinking, he was still playing the game but I couldn't hear him breathing. I heard only myself breathing. More and more a case of wheezing. I thought he was pretending to be dead. My own breathing was effected by his weight and my attempts at shouting were futile. Just a few squeaky wheezes were possible. As he stiffened my exhaustion increased, the task of shifting him became impossible, and his staring motionless expression scared the shite out of me. His right arm had lodged down the side of my bed and acted as an extra restraint. Like a strap. My wheezing shouts for help went unheard as they were not audible as far as the bingo hall down the road where my fat mother had deposited her fat arse for the evening. And not another soul was around. No one else was in the house. No one else was expected until after the bingo which was always late, and then all the talking made it later. My only thought was that I was going to die from the tremendous weight squeezing the life out of me. I could only take small, short breaths but they seemed after a while to come with ease if I didn't struggle. And then I thought of worse scenarios, the mother winning the big bingo prize and dying of shock and no one coming here for hours or even days. Maybe I would starve if no one came at all. The sense of panic grew and grew. He stopped there and paused for a thought and to take an asthmatic breath. *You see, I know about trapped. I know it well.*

It probably would have disturbed him to know that I never really thought about his situation at all. I didn't care a shite about his world as a child, about his fat father and his bizarre death. I wished the child McGraw had died and his breath had been extinguished on bingo night. That would have been the jackpot. I didn't ask what happened next, something he expected to hear.

11.

Guided privately, but by no means unavailable, with total disregard for McGraw's tale of woe, I sang in my head, *I dream of Shubert with the greasy grey hair* to the tune of, *I dream of Jeanie with the light brown hair.* Then it all fell into place. Attention applied to a neat parting, parted in participation with wig wax and a stainless steel, stiletto handled comb, ploughing a widening path through deep scurf drifts to despair. Hair was where it started.

A revelation. An occurrence in nature. Disclosing what was common to us and what to the intuition, by the grace of God expressed from his far side, was essential. Far from the fact, far from S is not P and the rest of it. The plane of correspondence into which each spirit that participates plunges. Here, in this restricted collaboration was an affected capacity, a modal essence affirmed in existence as some degree of power or other, determined to endure as a mutilated old man. In expurgated becoming, he was almost the primitive self. But not quite the thing-in-itself, not yet. Nor until death, once more, an actual essence. Nothing is lost with the loss of existence.

Advancing in thought in the direction of the whole of old Shubert, the lodger, in my mid-teen head (closer to childhood than his, you'd think), in his primitive presence or out of it, I saw all his sides, insides, outsides and backsides. Splitting sides or taking sides, I anointed him with forms of the general and artificial. Insignificance in the main, his needs, thus leading to the comparison and identification with lowly creatures. In all this I saw clearly McGraw going the way of old Shubert, and in and through Shubert I came to understand more of McGraw. They were a similar class of men, unsavoury and both on the trail of sweetness.

From her moral crow's nest mother McGladdery, old Shubert's landlady, was always on the lookout for such a class of man, to set apart, and subordinate to her provocative magical powers. When old Shubert came into the place of her personalised ethology, the commanding idiom of the louse was yet again unleashed. A jargon that soon had him on the short leash. He was more like a louse than a man was the drift. Like the louse his needs were few, his capacities maybe even fewer. Draughtless warmth, the sniff of the bitter draught and the sleeping draught, enough to float a ship out of dry dock. *He'll soon feel the draught of my temper, the cut of my tongue,* said the mother.

Empty skite was the cutting utterance confined to the occasion of stoking the fire. He hovered empty skite-like somewhere in the ashes that she prodded with the poker. *Skitter,* when she had the holy wind in her pinafore sails pegging out his washing. There he was before her in skitter capacity, desperately denying his weak bowels, in his linen on the line. She dreamed, on occasion, of stringing him up. She believed in a form of Biblical justice for lousy tenants. His garret constituted the condemned man's cell. His rights were limited by his inability to keep at bay what disagreed with him, largely through a life of failed trickery in the presence of harmful company in public houses all over the south of the city. *Keep your seed basket clean,* she warned him, standing sentinel each time he entered her front door. The meaning of this puzzled him, opening up to him all the dark corners of his own mind to find the answer.

Was he a man or a louse? I thought on that species of theme for thick slices of time. On the compositions, corruption and capacities of the being in question. *Define what he is*, said Frankie the wise older brother. *List his simple ways. And what he is capable of.*

Two quasi-adequate thoughts came rushing to mind. Simple and backward like a child. Backward also as he's always looking back. Over his shoulder or into his past, I said. *And shifty, on account of his sneaky disposition.*

Is that the extent of it? said the brother. *What about annoying, daft, vain, ungrateful, sly, sleaked, cowardly, lazy, dishonest, desperate, deceitful. But shifty is good, his unshifting nature in our house. Nothing can shift him out of that bolthole and burrow that is his rented room except the wee mother. But listen, it is the universal shift that we are forced to recognise. Are we all not of the same nature? As Nature is one individual. When is a horse not a horse?* he continued, a variation of the same question on countless other occasions. *When the horse is the one you're thinking of*, he answered without a lot of delay.

Occasionally, in flashes, at a distance from his inquisitional gaze, I saw the sense of this horse business when I had a thought of old nag Shubert. When is a Shubert not a Shubert? When he isn't *what* he is. Nor *that* he is. Shifty Shubert the shite stoker. Stoker first class from his British navy days. Here he harboured a grand grudge.

Being captivated by this or that class of a man, then the concrete class of things, will lead inevitably to the singular meaning of things, disclosed the brother.

That was my tormented world. Always misunderstanding. A never ending pursuit of agreements between thought and what was said to be real. Did it matter what was real? *They* said so. And that *they* said so led to thinking of language itself and what it is to say something. The immediate effect was to slip into a stern silence, as a gaoler imprisoning my own utterances.

Then the internal strife. Endless queries. Rhythms of reasoning. Slippages. Mutilations. Of things close and things distant, inside and out, fast and slow. The significant sides of things. Self-searching, digging, soul-searching, mining my own business down a shaft of darkness until I was in possessed of some sort of lunacy. An out-of-this-city numinous knowing. Deserting devotion to this parish of certainty.

Hermeneutics, Frankie said. *How to avoid misunderstanding. Say thanks to Mr Schleiermacher.*

Get the facts right.

No! Facts! No facts! That string of nonsense. Fact totem. There are no facts, he declared. *A fact is a mutilation, observations to abstraction. It's all about devotion to the common notion. You can't go far wrong there!* What was he trying to mean? *And beware of the confession of a clear consciousness.*

Ah, the wind bloweth, bullshitted the blithe Pastor Prebble in his Pentecostal bull pit. *Breathe on me breath of God! Fill me with life anew.* So I may observe a class of facts and a class of acts. *Beware a class of facts as a class of acts. F-acts,* said my brother, *as they require the fact of the faith act.* The common currency of acts in this place permeated by desire, saturated by striving. As it is Inside and out of the fine fusty old house in a fine old tree lined and well defined street. The clouded home in Belfast, the city of semi-darkness, unenlightened in nineteen seventy-two. Now *there* was a right time. Time of the hunters and hyenas. Not just the habitual hunt and ritual slaying but a rewriting of the rule book, and a commitment to carry on as defined in these new ways.

Here (or there) on the long night of nights in July seventy-two, a process of being. Some may say an event, as if this was merely a matter of confining the mind to the observable. That would be a deceiving diversion of the horticultural variety.

Internally there was a pot on the gas stove heating up tea to strong dark brown brew. Intensively cohesive, like stew. Extensively disturbed and distributed over the healthy blue flame. A reheating. Oddly enough, a process called stewing. Not to everyone's liking. Some turned their noses up at it. A taste of Ulster. A sturdy plantation man's substance. Like a thick fry to stuff the stomach and grease the joints. Thick heels of excessively buttered bread double-parked on a nearby plate.

In the vicinity of the stove two mugs lingered, the natural and the artificial, both definitively part of the arrangement. One with aged finger curled and ready to insert in a nook in the other. The other, with a little drop of milk in the bottom, prepared for its treacly fill. A piece of crockery that was a shrine around which aged hands clung and lips reverently approached. A cheap relic, caressed as if its dynasty were Ming. But it waited and waited. As did the other mug, Old greasy haired shite stoker first class Shubert, stranded momentarily between room temperature and boiling point. A class act according to a dubious particular matter of fact, a dodger, empty inside and on a quest near enough to the midnight hour. Having sneaked down the many stairs in his crap carpet slippers, like the offcuts of actual carpets, he waited. He believed in revelation, which has a lot to do with waiting, but he was old and nothing yet had been revealed except the powerful weaknesses of the body, his poverty and age. Meanwhile, he held on to his faith. In his general waiting he boozed and slept. In all this he was alone, experiencing large amounts of the decomposing loneliness and little solitude where singularly a man could, it was said, sense the numinous.

I remembered *Lonely Are The Brave* with smiling Kirk. The funny business of a man on a horse on the run who also stood his ground. But Shubert lacked courage to take a stand, that would give him steady legs. He also lacked a horse. *(When is a horse not a horse? When is courage not courage? When you are stuck without a horse?)* And a wide open landscape to escape to on the back of it. Like the desert that Christ occupied alone without a horse. *What did Christ have that Shubert lacked?* asked Frankie. *Speed,* I answered in a flash. A flash of the funny for us both.

The shite stoker first class was also forgetful, and on the verge of being forgotten. He failed to remember but he also failed to forget. His things unforgotten were those that should have been consigned forever to the past. Not through repression but through repentance. Repentance is forward looking. Forward looking on your bended knees. To an explicitly low horizon. Here in this world he was in danger. His unforgotten past was all encompassing, it held him to account at every turn, and so, he had never been in possession of a true future, but he was truly in the future plans of others. The trackers and laughing boys.

Was this the essence of his sadness? Was this the essence of the general sadness that surrounded us all in this place of buck stupidity? Buck stupid Belfast. This was indeed a place that proudly resurrected on a daily basis the painful past. A place totally unable to forget and remember appropriately.

Shubert remembered a whole multitude of his childish ways and preserved them presently in magnificent magnitude. Like his elevated need for sweetness. Such a need also defined his lowly nature and pointed to the simplicity of conditions required for others to know the course of his actions. Frankie said that such a simple mind could be unravelled like the antics of apes in Belfast Zoo. *Sweet preserve in his mental nature reserve,* he chanted.

The old shite stoker was at the mercy of his needs when he contemplated sweet tea. He achieved not even a diplomatic detachment from it to animate other human refinements. The mother was satisfied in herself that there was a power for her in such a separation and denied him a union with it, so, deploying the rotational tactic, the sweet thing he craved was hidden here and there far from his loafing grasp.

Knowing all the time the latest location of the Silvery Spoon two pound white sack he still mumbled, *Where is the white granule?* With the empty mug ready and waiting on the work top counter, his body brought forth to him certainties, and as his affection for his body was profound, it telling him of meteorological developments practically on the hour, he had a vision in his feet which took him to where he could lay his hands on the booty. He knew also, from a secondary form of certainty, from the informer he had recently enlisted according to blackmail rules, that he'd be on a pig's back at the midnight hour on such and such a night.

On this night, in the mother's kitchen, in expected solitude, knowingly free from a certain overseeing frightening feminine presence, as the informer had reported according to the rules, he seized the opportunity to locate the crystal substance, and liberally release its sweet, destructive properties, the evidence of that all too obvious in the old mug's empty grate. There was hardly a greater joy for him than when this sweetness was at his disposal. It is the joy-passion, passive in its routine recognition of what is common to a body and the affecting substance. Not quite yet, however, the active joy of the common notion.

White-stained enamel stained with the bubbling brew's excess, shoved up through the spout, spitting and sizzling on contact with the blue flame, staining the stainless enamel. Stains on stains and the remains of stains. And stained on the mind of the old fool, an unmoveable, unsightly blemish, part and parcel now of his whole mental weave. His mind with her in mind. His mind within her mind. Without a doubt the universal mother with its powerful casting shadow. A dedicated member of her class of women and mothers. Though the old goat only knew one instance of this sort, he, in truth, in accordance with the common notion, had to know them all. A blemish of fierce malignancy, a threatening incendiary of feminine force. A frightening blot, small and squat, heaving in perpetual temper, with a mind equally contaminated by ugly stains. From a menagerie of meagreness she came. That was a truth that staggered her. From an extended abundance of old Belfast poverty. Knowing herself in her own relation as being from the very same tribe as her lodger.

He took his lousy stand there in her scullery with the weary stoop of age. The lazy stoop of stupidity. The rooted stoop of fear. This animal shrinkage to avoid detection. Never a man bolt upright since his ship stoker days. A vestige in string vest of the primitive cower. The heavy burden of cowardice? The louse within him edging to full exposure. There *it* is, the non-human within, slinking down under the sink with half-sunken hopes of revealing the firm rounded and weighty sack and spooning the contents in heaps, into the waiting warm brown liquid, until there rose a moistened peak, ready for substantial stirring. Total immersion from above, fluidising the solid grain. Matrimonial in modal composition. The coming together in harmonious union. The new communion.

With Shubert's descent into this increasingly single-minded craving in mind, Frankie found his form for composing the profane liturgical ditty, elevating the shrinkage, the deceasing by significant decrease into non-form, beyond its deserved capacity. *Drink ye all of it, ye all from timeless cup. Romance the pouting lips, treat the trembling tongue. Sup and slurp the last reluctant drops. Employ all the power of lips and tongue to satisfy the expectant senses.*

Shubert, aware of his diminished reputation, demanded his due respect. *There is a bullet with my name on it*, he said to a heedless house. The turncoat who could do with a new suit of clothes. He had a history, internal to the place. Traitorous acts at a time and in a place poured out like the raging dysentery in those days of disorder. Accused by the tight motivated mouths of those who waited in his wake in dark ghetto doorways for their moment. In the event of his death the cause would be known. But no respect was heading his way, especially from the mother. *Objectum specificat actum.* He was the immanent object of her hate, her disgust, and even of her fun and the action she took in connection with this object was expressed in a legalism that knew no bounds. Laws to moralise, to prohibit, to immobilise action, to turn blind eyes and bind thought.

They're after me out there, he muttered on the threshold to be heard.

Behold the body, whispered the brother to be heard selectively, *aspects of an ambiguous arse. The brute backside. A truly surprising thing. Doesn't know if it's coming or going or where it belongs.*

Those mad Fenian fuckers with their fake Fenianism, the shite stoker first class Shubert announced, out of an unclear conscience, to be heard. His own Fenian loyalty an outmoded form. But he wasn't heard.

The lodger simply obeyed as the lodger must, in most things but not all. The infant need and his simple existence constituted his main resistance. A diminishing opposition. His boasting persisted only as sounds to the ears all around, like a child's invitational gurgling and cooing, but not even that, as it was despised and rejected. Or like the still, small voice of God that was nothing more than breath. In his case bad, boozy breath that would re-ignite the dying embers of a burning bush. *The Lord is not in the wind,* said my brother, *nor in the fire.*

The pastor says it's in the wind that bloweth, remember? I said.

He's full of the wind that old bloater, retorted Frankie. *If you listen to him carefully, to his body, you can hear the fart of folly.*

The blood boiled in the mother's veins, the *materia* of her motive and emotion, at the old skitter's resistance to her law. Regular ejection of the nonconformist from the household was the mainstay of her sanity and a particular joy in itself. In his removal there was a reverie, as there was in his inevitable reinstatement.

His ejections, when they came, were particularly unwelcome when middle of the night bed warmth, sheathed in body-hugging longjohn snugness, positioned foetally with hands nestling in the nest of testicles, was unscrupulously withdrawn.

With no warning, a barrage of the unpleasant, an invasion of unsettling and disturbing opposite sex sense data arrived at his lodger's door to fill his immobile mind with terror. A terror that appeared to find manifestation only in the usual infantile, pre-imaginative, psychical expressions.

Simultaneously, the brightness of an unshaded light bulb, the all encompassing draft of wintry cold, no matter the season, the harsh verbal scringings filtering through the well waxed ear, added to the overall sense of vulnerability. With a flick of her finger, with a turn of her wrist, the anonymity offered by darkness and the protection of the bed covers was removed. There he was, revealed. The sloth-like body exposed in a flash.

The swinging light bulb and the swinging fist. The contorted face of feminine anger. The mouth of flexibility mouthing the inflexible message. A gathering of images and ideas all generated by the one forceful utterance with an unmistakable meaning. The little fat finger, pointing the way down and out was unwavering. Like a signpost. OUT!! Out of that bed. Out of that room. Out of this house. Out of her life. No words of his, no appeal to old man frailty, or family loyalty, no old self-pitying look or begging posture, no bended knee or praying plea could shake her resolve. Not even one of the massed ranks of holy relics on the bedside table constituted a power of assistance. They would all be swept into a plastic supermarket bag by the signpost arm, and, like him, with him, once more, be homeless.

Where does he get his idols, I asked.

In his idle mind, said the brother. *Those idols are really in his head, to combat his factory of fear. When the boozer dozes in his bed. A bulldozer. Full of sleepy bullshite.*

But the old mug Shubert, soon reinstated and on a pig's back, and failing yet again to remember, continued to search for the sugar. What was stewed tea without it?

Late one night, in one of his previous temporary tenures, in a deserted house that I was left to guard, I found him where he should not have been, on the third landing, one short of his destination, grounded, flat on his back and confounded. Unconscious to the core. Gurgling from his throat and snorting from the snout. Demanding of himself a power to stand. Denouncing the unwilling body that correspondingly, in its fallen flatness, denounced an unwilling mind. He rose and fell repeatedly, like the chinned pugilist deprived of firm ankles and knees.

I was still young enough to feel the full pull of fear, its objective power driven on by the untrustworthy immature imagination. The Devil's best friend. The primitive *experientia vaga*. Old dark death near at hand in an increasingly faltering, at times barely detectable breath. The struggle between life and death, sameness and difference, going on. Death as a thing of opposition leaping onto life from a dark corner in a house of darkled corners. Was the Devil lurking? Or a murdering Fenian foe that the old goat had talked of?

There he lay clutching in his rigid right fist a mug, tilted to the amplitude of the horizontal landing to reveal the tan sludge of a sugary mixture, whilst that invisible demon death mounted him.

Behind the croaking and choking I thought I heard the sound of my name rumbling forth from the depths of his weak bowels, as if uttered by an occupant of the polis of Hades.

Seamus, your secret is not safe, it farted. Within the indefinite compass of *temps vécu,* hidden in my own dark corner, from where I spied him, I considered the shortening of the man's breath with a handy silky smooth ligature that I carried in my trouser pocket. So he could not speak the thing he had over me from a prior accidental encounter.

I paid a high price for not, on that single occasion, simply turning a key, and locking the door behind me. Inside my sister's bedroom on the second landing, where I confidently considered solitude to be my own, Shubert, in a stocious swoon, not subject to voluntary control, stumbled powerfully through the unsecured portal to gaze, with his enlarged and momentarily sober epistemic eye, upon the bare *corpus delicti,* arresting its perfectly judged velocity and rhythm, destroying the cerebral and corporeal cohesion of the discerning single thought-act, the satin scarf knotted neatly in a pussy bow on the neck.

Reduced by the interruption almost to a state of rest, to a paralysis of the discerning thought and its act, the act and its thought, I was enslaved in an instant by the sluggish and mutilated mind of the of old shite stoker first class. I was a slave to this flattened curiosity before me. A slave to a slave. To him who was no longer even able to encounter himself, who, in his own special relation wailed endlessly at his lifetime of misfortune, accusing all around of being fools when all the time he was the fool, the subordinate tied to a consciousness in collusion with confusion and compromise who came into conflict with every encounter and registered each time a new instance of ruin that depleted any power that he possessed in his singular modality.

Here, just one faltering step inside the sister's room, he registered one small victory out of which he thought he could act to extricate himself from the results of a lifetime of becoming separated from the act. In an ocean of ontological indolence this one instance of mastery persuaded him that he had retrieved the situation, when in fact he had only witnessed his own meagre moment of joy, a purely transitive event in his thought, a mere imagination, a joy restricted in its power to a passion as he was not the cause of it.

In my own reduced relation, I surrendered, for an indefinite duration, to *his* sad cause. Here was a rudimentary rule of three, Shubert, sugar and me, each sucked into a unique domain of destructive opposition. In my case, cruelly drawn back from a point of conversion, from the liberation offered in the sister's room, to take an unsteady stand in a disagreeable relation to him, incorporated into his corrupt constitution as a faster function, as his eyes and ears distributed where his could not go. As his informer. The duration of this status, owning to the old empty skite's folly, was calculably short. The capacity used to act for him was as easily used to act against him.

What quantity of a while it was no one could calculate, but on the long night of nights, anticipating the inevitable approach of sweet communion, when the fire had all but gone out, Schubert headed for his caper in Mother McGladdery's kitchen.

Open you lugs, whispered Frankie from his bed across from mine, on hearing carpet slippers drag across the landing outside our bedroom door and plant themselves on the stairs. *Define what the old empty skite is now in this moment of unfolding tragedy. He'll be heading for his own kind, restoring his meek actual essence. Well done Seamus, this may be the end of it. A pig's back awaits us.*

On the fall of a silent note, also of incalculable duration, which involved no further sound of the dragging of the slippers or creaking of the stairs under the weight of the old skitter, whose shrinking powers marginalised everything indifferent in mind to the caper ahead, the ears of Frankie and me listened out for the recommencement of audible unpleasantries between a thing in its own relation and another thing in its own relation in their inner effort to establish the governance of their fictional strengths one over the other. There was hardly anything more amusing in the *facies totius universi* and had to be seen and heard.

From a deep shadow in an adjoining room, of incalculable size but able to hold both me and Frankie in a hidden capacity, enough size, said Frankie to ease my doubts, to hold the immediate and mediate infinite modes that determine all things as existing, we watched the antics in the scullery.

It just took one lazy thought of her from him for her to be there before him. Owing to the magnitude of concentration given over to the sugar shovelling caper, the conscience-stricken stoker was spared thinking about the logical considerations of the mother's appearance. Neither the contingent or necessary in causation. She was just given to him as present, but a continuing present, as, sadly for him, she was no fleeting particular. Nor was he fleeting for her.

She had emerged at speed from an under-stairs cloak room that led directly to the kitchen. Coming to him from behind, the treacly brew in the precious mug with all its invisible sweetness was snatched from his grasp and held tantalisingly with feminine fat finger firmness. A firmness that quivered with mounting anger. Vacant old stoker hands moved to pleading a case but the cause was yet again ineffectual. No mercy here, no last minute reprieve. The punishment was coming. The tea, the woman, the turning fat wrist and the forward thrust with the precursory, *if you bloody well want sugared tea I'll give you bloody sugared tea*, before the action.

And so it was. The aftermath. Standing in a slouch, stupid, spluttering, licking leaves, liquidic leer under flattened, shiny thatch, now with no parting, Shubert once again, and for the final time, resumed his station out there in the madness, beaten and more bitter than ever, and never to speak the words against me. Apart, unconnected, his difference clear, but so too his sameness, all the same, he was sent out to a kind eternity.

12.

If I had only been able to embrace the *idea* earlier I would have been on a pig's back. If I had have stayed on at school, I was told, things in my understanding might have been different also, but school was a place of useless questions and useless tasks, one useless one after another, and it was school that was partly responsible for leading us all astray. Someone says that we already know all the answers but what we don't know are the questions. Like in church we know God already.

In my unconscious quest for the questions, I had discovered that not all questions are valid, what was given at school was not in any way related to learning and that the concrete idea was completely missing. What was put in its place was the abstract idea. In maths, for example, the idea of *kind* was missing in the teaching of simple numeracy. The abstract concept was all over the place, leading us all to self destruction, all derived from the fixation with and entanglement in the facts.

Alan the listener seems happy with my detailed recounting of Pastor Prebble's sermon on Nicodemus, an account of no factual merit, he says, but he is now sitting with Spinoza's *Ethics* in his lap looking dejected.

Look at this, he murmurs with the book open. *Save the phenomena. That's what they say isn't it? This man is all about logic. But what's this?* Flicking through the pages he produces a sheet of paper and unfolds it.

What he unfolds is an old English homework essay of mine. *Pick one member of your family and describe them in a few paragraphs in an unusual way.* Use your imagination we were told, not just a list of facts. My mind immediately jumped upon our mad old lodger Shubert (not strictly a family member, but steadfastly present), an unusual man I could describe in an unusual way. My brother Frankie said he was a mad mode but to understand such a modality was a way to begin to understand the essence of things. Everything but God is a mode, he said. Modes are the most dependent things in existence, they can neither be by themselves nor conceive by themselves. The infinite modes wander through existence, their movements as bodies governed by motion and rest and their thoughts by the infinite intellect. Substance, Attributes, Modes, make up the holy Spinozan trinity, the Godhead, but God is even so far beyond them he is unthinkable, except unto himself.

I knew little of this but the mode Shubert I did know and so was a good place to start. In fact, Spinoza and old Shubert were not unlike I thought, both hidden away in their attics, one full of thinking the thought and one full of drinking the draught. In the end, armed with my Frankie's copy of the Ethics, and some brotherly assistance, I (we) embarked on an exercise in total madness.

Essay Title: *My old Uncle Shubert. Mass murderer of modes.*

Shubert exists! Just. As a decomposing mode. All modes, infinite in kind, are either composing or decomposing. Shubert is latterly of the latter category reflected in his incessantly sorrowful mood. Yet all modes are the product of God and have no existence apart from God, so even the decomposing being that is Shubert could claim an ontological amplitude corresponding to that of God in his infinitely expressive attributes of body and mind. Modes are not mere fictions nor are they facts. A mode is never a mode by itself, if it were it would never die, once in existence it would continue along an everlasting path, but like this it would never *be anything*. What causes a mode to die and paradoxically *to be something* is another mode. It is my guess that Shubert is a mass murderer of other modes as I could only see his decomposing spirit, as no other mode that comes into contact with him experiences composed joy, only decomposed sadness. Which means that the family, a mode in itself, at one time a powerfully healthy mode, is made unhappy in his company. Shubert's cell-like room is itself a mode, an extended compost heap of decomposition, and in the modular interaction the affective smell is sufficient, not only to remove the appetite to nourishment but to install a desire to be in a state of unconsciousness in which there is the possibility of insubordination.

A mode however need never be satisfied with being merely a mode, a higher form of being beckons insofar as it loves and does not hate. A mode should hate hate, as hate is the greatest poison known. *We endeavour to destroy the man we hate,* said Spinoza, and if we hate ourselves we seek our own destruction. In guilt we see our own hate for ourselves. Shubert sees this clearly and desires to destroy himself with the demon that is drinking booze. But as the mind of a mode is not absolutely destroyed with the body there is hope for old Shubert yet. But hope is an uncertain joy and Shubert is uncertain about enjoying it. He also isn't allowed into the parlour.

The End

I didn't want to put The End as I felt in the flow of some higher state of mind. Like in a churchly charismatic rapture. The essay caused considerable ruffling of pedagogical feathers. First there was the doubt I was actually the author. Then, *This tells me nothing about this man Shubert,* shouted Hardiman the English master who I thought of as a wanker moron of a mode. His mark was an E- for impertinence.

Where did you find this mad language? he said. I had no words for him.

13.

Me and McGraw. Odd men out. In and out of each other's minds. Each with our own ideas of the other, no greater than those of creatures that strive to raise themselves above the given conditions of their knowledge and awareness but fail to achieve clarity above illusion. This was a laughing crying place. Like that London railway platform. Trapped modally, I was disposed neither to tears nor to laughing, though both were equally possible as a result of an absence of power. In this troubled place it was never certain who had power of the self, who had power over who, for power here meant a limited congress of wills and desires, submissive to the appetites large and small. And what moved them in the various directions was the blind consciousness of desire which they mistook to be free action.

Here I was hollowed out, a superficial structure, all effort it seemed determined for me. I was a slave to everything that happened. Not even a slave who knew he was a slave. A form of madness as all that was manifest was an immediate awareness of passing from one state to the other without ever really knowing anything.

Now, in our small movements in the empty yard, contemplating caution and entertaining desire, a pressing weakness was upon me, and so an immense sadness, but surprisingly also a fleeting sense of joy, which indicated that within the risk, attached to the danger, there was still the possibility of power, though joy itself may only be a reflection of a friendly affect, a present, pleasant happening. It may also mean an adequate active affect, a power of acting. It also pointed to the notion that an *individual thing itself* is not one body but many.

I saw old McGraw before me but I also saw the young boy McGraw trapped under a big fat quickly-hardening collapsing dead da. I almost laughed at that in the midst of all the fleeting fictions that presented themselves. Something of a laugh was there all right. I also almost laughed at my idea of the lad Sticky McGraw going about his business in the world. An abundantly bloated specimen of a lad with the unique distinction of being friendless, and who was always at the wrong end of the grotesque humour of the unfriendly. *His da died on him,* they would scream in his face, *died on top of him and the peelers thought his da died trying to fuck him.*

McGraw had the expression of a distressed child, reflections on his trapped story continued to rake up sorrow out of the depths of his painfully engorged guilt-ridden soul. Gone the gunfire now. No screaming and shouting or the noises of pain. No cruel laughter. Nothing but that hiss in the ears, swelling inside the head. Not a blissful hiss. We looked around in stupid fashion. Stupidly staring directly at the stillness. Nothing of a noise in the place that made people deaf. The father had slowly gone deaf but hadn't realised, as he shouted at everyone at close quarters and in conditions of perfect quietness. The brother Frankie and me spluttered up our moist delight in splendid appreciation when we were witnesses to the startled looks in receiving faces of *the shout,* as we called it. But everyone barked at each other in this place, to be heard over the noise of the machinery, and it was also considered manly to shout.

I'm having bad notions here, bad notions, McGraw declared in an uncomfortably close whisper.

When is a horse not a horse? I muttered. McGraw wasn't slow in looking puzzled. He was noticeably more nervous with the puzzlement. He was eager to increase our speed of movement to safety in conformity with the increasing speed of his nervousness. The nervous speed stands in a bad kinetic relation to other speeds and is destructive of possible form. It also has uncertain direction.

He led me back more slowly passed the despatch office, then on to the time office and the front gate passing down one side of the deserted articulated lorry. The usually busy main despatch office at our backs was eerily uninhabited. No timekeeper Lundy in the time office before us either. Maybe he travelled to safety via his legless mode of movement just in time.

The closed main gate seized the attention from beyond the front of the lorry. From beyond the gate renewed outside bellows informed us that we were far from safety. Shifty fellows with urgently shuffling shoes announced their presence on the other side of the lorry. McGraw stopped dead, but not dead enough. I was right in his rear, looking at his big back, and thinking of his demise.

We lowered ourselves and peeped under the lorry to the other side. There was a good selection of dirty and confused footwear turning and pointing one way then another. Not friendly footwear either. Flighty footwear. Whispering of the heavy sort was going on, passing under the lorry and into our ears which strained to hear the content.

Did you hear that, said McGraw. *They said they're going fishing?* He was more or less just mouthing now and expecting me to read his lips.

They're not going to catch us so don't fucking worry, said one of the shifty crew on the far side of the lorry. *We're not fish to be caught.*

When is a fish not a fish? I whispered.

When it's in a fucking bakery, said the vexed McGraw.

We edged forward to the time office hoping to escape through that route, but met face to face with a shifty crew. Five in number. The number of a kind, I thought, the shifty crew kind, of the shifty crew universal. A thought that I repeatedly expressed to Alan the Listener.

It was an uncomfortable encounter as there were no faces to read, only eyes behind dark green balaclavas, the kind the mother called it a hood. Knitted hoods were feared garments when we were wee. The itching discomfort on the neck was almost unbearable and you had the look of an utter imbecile in one. These were all young men in front of us, by the given lean build of their bodies and the energy in their voices.

They breathed heavily behind their woolly masks. They'd clearly been running around the place looking for an escape route. They had used the lorry to ram the front gates but had failed. They couldn't get the vehicle in reverse and there was no momentum to the ramming, just pushing the gate which was useless. Now urgency prevailed upon them. The front offered no way out we were told, not even through the time office, and the army were all over the front of the building. McGraw told them that he knew another way out, and pointed in a weak fashion to the frail gate at the far corner of the yard. The one we had just been looking through at the B-Special Constabulary Christmas pantomime. So we ploughed the whole cut back to the gate in single file.

It's locked, said McGraw, as we approached it. It hardly mattered as a laced-up heavy, black boot soon disposed of it with a single kick. There wasn't a soul about when we stepped outside into the misty darkness of Raphael Street.

14.

McGraw and me, odd men out with the shifty crew. There is a film called *Odd Man Out. D'you know it?* I ask the Listener. *A blinder,* he says back. I tell him that I first watched it when I was a wee lad and sick with a swine of the flu. The worst flu for years everybody said. Everyone was getting it and were laid out flat with it. My brother Frankie was taken into hospital with it. He nearly died the mother said proudly. Nobody could get upright because of the vertical vomiting. The body just got out of control. Now it was my turn. A few days off school soon turned into a few weeks.

A blinder alright. It's a film and a half is Odd Man Out. It's set in Belfast but not a Belfast film. It's really a holy film. Full of mysterium tremendum The numinous. And the noble and courageous. James *Nicodemus* Mason is the star. He's all over the place looking for salvation. It was made by people who didn't know Belfast but somehow grasped a wee bit of the spirit of the place. Maybe because they paid no attention to the facts of the place.

Oh and how you hate the facts, said Alan the Listener.

Half truths, I replied.

Feeling small and ill on a lumpy brown settee, in my half delirium and trembling, I remembered everybody in the film getting a big soaking in the Belfast rain. They got that right. But there was also a really sunny winter day with not a sign of rain. And snow at the end. The black blood on soft whiteness.

James Mason is a criminal running away from the peelers, but you soon forget he's a criminal. What relief when he always stays just out of reach from his enemies. All the streets are narrow cobbled affairs. Small clans of children cluster around areas of weak artificial light playing their games. Couples arm in arm are heading off to a pub or a dance hall. Electric trolley buses with their internal lights and external sparks brighten up the end of every street. There are unusual streets just as I remember them, adjoining streets running parallel one to the other but not on the same level. Access from one to the other are via steep steps with railings. Street corner shops are lit up and busy until late hours, the hucksters making a good living charging double the price on everything that no one seems to mind paying.

I sweated in front of a blazing fire. The mother was seated beside me, comforting me with her fat fingers running through my thick, wavy hair and occasionally placing her cold palms on my forehead. How come that bald Bilko the barber interferes with this pure pleasure? His fingers replacing the mother's. His laugh appearing before me. The old men on the waiting bench too.

I rested my feet on a stone hot-water bottle. Part of the time I thought I was in the car, on the way back in the dark from a day out at the beach. Lying almost asleep on the back bench seat watching the street lights flash by.

The mother excitedly pointed out places in the film familiar to her. She encouraged me to get up and look, so I raised my sick body up time and time again to see. Just for a few seconds, until I felt my whole body registering immense discomfort.

There's the big Albert Clock, she said. *Look at it, look!* Up again I came. But in my weariness I soon slid down again on the sofa with a vague notion of the big bright clock on a tower, a floating clock with a massive tick, ticking away in the continuous dampness. *Does it never rust*, I asked the mother. She laughed at me as if I was stupid. But I was just sick. Sick of the palsy. *Is this is what palsy is like?* I mumbled weakly. *No, that is only in the Bible.* Nobody had the palsy in these days of ours. We had plenty of feverish delirium and in my many bouts of it I thought of people called Paul having the palsy. Starting with St Paul.

Back in extended delirium on the sofa with my mother, I smuggled Hardy Kruger from *The One That Got Away* into *Odd Man Out*, staggering around the frozen wastes of Canada, miles from the Albert Clock, trying to escape from the Allies in World War Two.

All damp in *Odd Man Out*, and all damp in Raphael Street with McGraw and me, odd men out with the shifty crew. McGraw leading them, the hooded men, somewhere, and was it in *Odd Man Out* that I could see the connection I made between Nicodemus and James Mason? He is the holy Irish terrorist Johnny McQueen, wounded with blood flowing for the cause of Ireland and on the run in the continuous damp and the dark. Did any of these fake fly fuckers have the spirit of Johnny McQueen in them?

15.

Now listen, Mr. Listener. This is it! This is it! This is it! I hadn't many more words in me to give him.

I lifted my up mine eyes to the hills from whence nothing of help cometh, but there were no divine hills, just the demonic dark and high solid shapes. We were in the power of the devilish fly boys with their hidden lying lips and deceitful tongues. Our feet shuffled with theirs, suffered and moved on. We skimmed the doorways of the flat fronted houses without forecourts, shoulders rubbing on seeping bricks. It had become apparent through the regular mumblings of McGraw that we were all heading for his house on Joy Street.

Here was a circumstance of inevitability, the sort of circumstance that I thought could be reversed through pure contemplation. Where time could be stopped, or held up indefinitely. Just think of every moment as it happens and nothing will happen. Or something else will happen in those frozen seconds to change the future inevitibilty into another future altogether.

The hooded fly boys pushed us odd men out along with seemingly nothing much more than their presence behind us. And the powerful weight of their weaponry. We edged out of the narrow back streets and onto the deserted main road looking out for peeler or army patrols on the move. I had been pushed forward to verify that the road was clear. It was the road to home if I chose. The main road to work that bypassed all those little streets that we were now emerging from. If I took off at full speed I would soon be out of sight. And free. Nothing they could do without alerting the peelers. Neither shoot nor shout nor chase. But, I didn't choose to go. I didn't shoot off to freedom and home. Restraining me was the new idea that home was not now the direction of freedom. A transition had taken place, a passage of modification, an increase in power that created an awareness that a choice possible, but also something in the circumstance that informed me that remaining in it was good and for the good. Not good in itself, but good because I desired it. There was an early presentation of composure. A tight duration that was constitutive of a mobilisation and extension of capacity.

We were soon across the main road and in another maze of hellishly miserable housing and my choice had been made. Here there was peace or the process of peace. The people of the place were at peace, all slumbering in their slum beds as we passed by their front doors. Henrietta, May, Catherine, Charlotte, Grace, Eliza. Only Joy to come. What of the McGraw women? Were they in these houses getting ready for us? Dolling themselves up for us? There were signs. We seemed to be going in circles.

McGraw and me were still in our loose-fitting whites which must have been remarkably distinct in the thorough darkness. I thought of Alec Guinness in *The Man with the White Suit*, running through the empty industrial streets of some northern English town in his indestructible white double-breasted suit. I thought of the lovely Joan Greenwood and her husky voice. McGraw was a mess in his whites, not at all like Alec Guinness. A mess of a man in a mess of a place. The mess that the fly boys wanted to possess and protect with their cause. There was the devil in them. What of the women? I wanted the devil in them. The women that were to change everything. If I lifted my eyes, lifted them off McGraw, I could see Henrietta under a hazy gas lamp—close to Joy. That sign.

Eventually we arrived at McGraw's place in Joy Street. From the very first step over the threshold opposition was fierce. Opposition that exists to test the courage. Opposition is death, there isn't death within us, only in other things. The awful smell and the unknown source of smell. The silence of the fly boys in the smell, the smell that is not death itself but fleeing life. I tried to abandon myself entirely to all that was present.

16.

The place without opposition was the church. The church now detached and in another place. But was it the place to find courage? If there was nothing to overcome where was the necessity to act courageously? *Back out in the world itself,* announced Pastor Prebble. Declaring your salvation to opposition outside the church. We wanted to be in the church but, once in, were pointed back to the world. Therein rested the reason for the testimony trail.

The father became one of the religious celebrities of the Ulster testimony trail, the *Faith from Fenianism* story. Telling it on the mountains, over the hills and far away. The story was perfected over the years to make it not only miraculous but amusing, amusing in the Lord, because the Lord was conceived, among many things, as a laughing Lord. It soon constituted a work of the purest imagination. Thus the testimony became an act, a performance, and the whole circuit of meeting places was just like a touring vaudeville show, with our little family troupe rolling into towns all over the Ulster province. The father was usually top of the bill. As we travelled the country roads in our old Austin A40, we all belted out "We'll Be Coming Around The Mountain When We Come," thinking it was a hymn, which it wasn't at all.

I was detained from other fruitful lines of want by a desperation to be top of the bill on the testimony trail one day and desired the holy ghost in high doses to get me there. One night when the spirit went berserk I thought, *Yes! This is it. It is there.* Reach out!

Don't think. Close your eyes and reach for it. Feel it pass into you. Pass through you.

In and through me I was me, but not me. I was the new me. Then the old me. People were keeling over all around the new and old me as the spirit passed through them like a physic. Chairs were moved to make large spaces for them to fall into. I squinted out of my closed eyes to see the holy mayhem. Women who hated suffering any indignity were being frighteningly undignified in huge doses with their short skirts flying up past their buttocks as they danced, quivered and fainted. I could view the buttocks without guilt because they were transubstantiated, holy buttocks, wobbly expressions of abandonment in the spirit. There was no shame with these earthly things when the spirit was moving. No shame because it was God's act and not theirs.

The Lord also extended the elders' hands, which felt, with exquisite precision, the tingling bodies as they fell into them. Hands worshipped. They were swinging in the air. Feet worshipped. They marched on the spot, stamping solidly swaying their bodies rhythmically to and fro. Tongues worshipped. Their babbling engulfed the sound waves. A queue of souls formed in the aisle to receive the hands that would mediate this that and the other spiritual gifts. There was the regular bunch of invalids who always queued for valid healing and there was the usual wild bunch who danced and grunted and hummed like mad African tribesmen without any sense of boundaries. The invalids were given a good firm laying on of shaking hands and were shaken to complete disorientation, until their earthly bearings were non existent. They were shaken with energising vigour until they believed they were healthier. If they weren't then there was always next week. If there was never an improvement it was surely due to their lack of true belief. They waited, as David the psalmist said on God's behalf. They should wait, until God inclined unto them.

The pastor and a couple of select elders had full license to interfere with the equilibrium and composed poise of anyone presenting themselves for prayer. Tight female hair perms were particularly at risk once those probing male hands set about their work. A derelict bird's nest appearance was evidence of successful laying on of hands. Neatly pressed and presented Sunday dresses and suits were turned by the holy mauling hands into wrinkled, dishevelled, undignified messes. People shivered like they were freezing cold. In went the air in a huge smooth suck and out it came in prolonged stuttering quivers.

At its height, the uproar resembled a riot in an madhouse. The whole house of God was shaking in its foundations. Before I knew it I was in amongst it all. My seated posture had become untenable with everyone else rising to their feet around me. I was convinced at that point that my buttocks were levitating off the seat, and that my legs, once on the floor, were out of my control and performing a soulful jig right into the epicentre of the commotion. I danced until I was purple in the face and feeling pleasantly dizzy. I began to speak with strange words. I murmured something nonsensical as I blew out the air and felt, at last, that I was possessed.

In the subdued assembly, in the tranquil aftermath, I felt that something had indeed altered. My slowly receding purple glow matched everyone else's. When the pastor said that the holy ghost had surely been in the midst, and had not yet departed, I blurted out an audible *praise God*. In the instant of its departure from my mouth I was cognisant of the withdrawal of my own capacity to speak, and of being a mere mouthpiece.

Later, no longer a mouthpiece, lying on my bed and looking up into the massive black mouth of doubt, nothing was certain. The alteration had been a deception. Had it? In what way? A deception of my own unbridled desire to have a testimony and be on the trail telling folk about my levitating buttocks, and being a mouthpiece.

I managed to get to sleep after being tortured and tormented for a good while, and when I woke with the notion that my right hand was good and holy and my left hand was still in the realm of the sinful world, I recalled the dream I had been having, a vague affair of being led by my black left hand into a dark cave. Within minutes of my body beating to the swiftest rhythms of consciousness, an favourable interpretation delivered me out of uncertainty. I had to be a much greater sinner in order to be a more powerful saint. I had to descend to the most profound and profane depths with the Devil himself, into the belly of hell that Jonah spoke of, make myself known, swearing as in the independence declaration, in the realms of the depraved, as the master loveless cunt, of the unique concrete universal cunt kind, for an indeterminate duration, before climbing out with the single good hand in the crack of that cliff. Up and up with devils at the heels who were none other than the pastor and elders and surprise surprise, old Shubert, all with their hands grasping and clawing and cleaving, all but old Shubert crying for the Lord to stop the climbing cunt. Old Shubert simply begged for booze or the currency to access it. That was the dream casting itself up in more detail, upsetting the rhythm of the consciousness and its attempts to bear witness to real matters on my way to Bilko's the winking barber, who would hold my tufts of wavy hair in his hand.

17.

There was a substantial, weighty element of waiting in Joy Street. A tide of anticipation in a room of substantial squalor off the main hallway. The waiting room of mammoth disorder. It was said that if you waited genuinely for God knowing you could never possess him, he would sooner or later possess you. As might the fly boys. We had been directed at gunpoint to sit silently and wait. On an old settee in the dark far from God. Odd men out sitting waiting for the fly boys to make themselves known.

Would they reveal something of themselves those fly fuckers? What of the women? Would they be part of the unveiling? In their newly applied mascara and lipstick. It seemed we were closer to divine revelation and rapture that the appearance of womanly form. What of movement? Activity? The absence of passivity was evident even though we waited in perfect stillness. Four fly boys sat themselves around the room, one was missing in another room, waiting there, as a lookout and listener, for opposing movement outside to stop. So this not-doing much told us little. We were all within ourselves, some at rest and some in commotion. What was expected was a different character of activity once interaction took place. A wave of words or particles of particular deeds. Would that character be shaped by a friendly relation or an unfriendly one? Apart from all this, from a distance, I would have thought that humour would be a prime mover to activity.

McGraw's stubble glistened with of sweat. His lenses were half-steamed up in the airless room. He rubbed them with a dirty finger but only succeeded in smudging them. Behind them he seemed to be contemplating a worrying near future. He footered around with his feet, shuffling the shoe soles in a restricted circle in the manner of stubbing out a fag. Like a man in the madhouse taking refuge in the habitual. Waiting. Waiting for the silence to break and the fly boys to break out and go their own way. The doorway was blacker than the rest of the room and through it came the missing fly boy. The lookout. The listenout. He switched the light on and we were all bathed in an orange glow. *Oh a Protestant sunset,* said he.

Straight across the room from where McGraw and me were sitting was a small table of the folding variety, covered in patterned oil cloth. Stacked on top with newspapers, magazines and records. Two fly boys raised themselves off the floor and sat on the chairs on either side of the table. The fly boy on his feet walked to the table and sifted through the pile of records. I attached to him the name Cleg as he seemed to be the man in charge. A cleg is the king of scary flies. If it was ever announced that a cleg was in our vicinity we'd all scarper for cover waving our arms to ward it off. With his back to us Cleg talked quietly to his inferior friends, looking back on occasions to McGraw and me with just a lazy turn of the head. A seated fly boy tapped his pistol barrel on the oil-clothed table top. *I knew it,* he said continuing to tap but with more force. Cleg was nodding. He walked to the wall to look at a picture that was hanging there. After several seconds of contemplation he returned to the table and whispered to the seated fly boys.

Are you crying? says the Listener.

A powerful joy and sadness, unraveling the idea and image. My voice quivers, my speech is entering the Listener's ears at an alarmingly increased speed and a tear is breaching the eye socket.

You are the boy, aren't you? said Cleg coming over to us and looking directly at McGraw.

What boy? replied McGraw after an awkward pause. Within the period of that pause Cleg had taken the few steps from the table to approximately no distance at all from McGraw. The Cleg crotch pressed ever firmer on McGraw's spectacles. I could hear the hinges of the glasses creak. The spectacle was almost enough to make me laugh. As was his answer, *What boy?* Daftness in an immensely serious circumstance. Like when my father kicked the piss-pot under my granny's bed when she was taking her final breaths. He leaned over to kiss her and his foot sent the full po-pot flying under the bed, rolling out the other side without the piss.

Cleg lifted the hood from the neck sufficiently to reveal his mouth. *Are you not heeding me? Now pay close attention to me. You are the boy, aren't you?*

I don't know if I am, stuttered McGraw, turning to me at the same time with a void look. He saw me through his smudged and steamed-up lenses, sitting crookedly on his face due to the damaged hinge. I imagined his perspective, a hazy, distorted orange world. I found it almost unbearable not to laugh.

Look at me, said Cleg. McGraw lifted his lazy eyes. *You don't know if you are? Do you know who you are?* McGraw seemed limp with genuine doubt, genuine fear. *You are McGraw, aren't you? What were you two on when we found you? The pair of you. What were you on? Him and you. On a good thing? On a pig's back? A wee corner of the lumber yard to do a lumbering job with your fine looking wee friend here, McGraw?* And so they knew him by name. *Tell me you know what I'm on about. Don't have me standing here looking like a prick without a cunt. Oh yes, you are the cunt. Don't be ashamed of your pleasures. What you want to do and what you do when you get what you want. If you were ashamed of your wants that would just piss me off. If you were ashamed of what you do to make you a happy man.*

Now, what sort of creature would that be? That would be a hypocrite. Us lads here just detest deceivers. Like being a traitor. A turncoat. We announce our cause to the world, we don't hide it.

With his hands clasped around the back of McGraw's skull Cleg pulled the McGraw face firmly into the fullness and intimacy of his groin and held him there in an almost passionate embrace. I tried to generate straight thinking in this curved confusion of orange light. About pleasure. About enjoyment. About enjoying pleasure, and desiring pleasure. About pleasure as sensation and pleasure located in the body, pleasure contained in an act of mind.. The names of pleasures, the claims of pleasures. Consciousness, the duty of consciousness was said to dominate the passions and herald the superiority of the mind over the body and protect the soul.

Isn't the body as important as the mind? Not more important but just as important?

Cleg took a step back. *Stand up, you perverted fucker, till I see the full of you! Get the fuck up now, shanker, you canker!* McGraw was slow to oblige. *On your feet, you foul fucker! You chicken shite. I want to see you on your feet like a man.* McGraw could barely shift his arse off the sofa. His body was disobedient. Next to him I felt the effort he was making to move. The grunts and groans. The creaky bones. The shaking of the sofa. The genuine incompetence of the struggle to his feet.

With McGraw now on his feet Cleg took a further step back. *Now drop your whites, quick!* said Cleg, *I have no time to fuck about. I want to see if you are enjoying yourself and not letting us know. I want to see if you have something for me to see. If you fancy me. So get them down.*

McGraw was obedient to both his own inner command and that coming from Cleg. But the act was overall one of submissiveness.

Aha! There it is boys. There it is. The triumphant body. Nothing hidden now. The bastard pleasure.

18.

To Alan the Listener, I say, *There is no singular thing in nature than which there is not a more powerful. Whatever one is given, there is another more powerful by which the first can be destroyed. That's from the man whose book you hold in your hand. Pleasure can be a sign of power but also weakness. The two seemed to be on show right in the Joy Street room. But never think you are invincible.*

Cleg stood in admiration of McGraw like an artist at the moment of his final brush stroke. The writer with his final word. Nothing of it is in truth final. In fact it just begins there. The mind concluding its imaginative process commences the act of contemplation. An act of affirmation. But McGraw was no work of art with his lower garments heaped around his feet. And Cleg was no artist.

Cleg turned to me. *What do you make of this old cunt buster? No cunt buster at all. A runt who shuns cunt. Cunts hold no interest for cunts like him. But he's giving me a nice compliment. Keep the home fires burning! What do you think of the bastard pleasure?* I didn't say a word. I took refuge somewhere else. In the divine ideas. The divine asylum. Back to notions of pleasure and madness in the house of God. The forms before me melted away. McGraw's bare arse, the fly boys, like real flies on an old bull's balls and caked crap arse, making him suffer. A real pleasure could not possibly be bad. We can however be mistaken about what is or is not a pleasure but a pleasure must, by its very nature, be good. Logic demands it, surely.

What was really going on here? Power? If pleasure is ultimately power, where we pass from lesser to greater states of perfection, then McGraw's state at this very moment was not to be considered a pleasure. He was meek McGraw who might inherit the world, but only if imperfection is the purpose of existence. He stood there in his fear and shame. Fear and shame, what are they? They are a sign of weakness, for fear is an uncertainty and uncertainty is an ignorance the strong cannot afford.

He's a masochist, said Cleg. *He's shite scared and shamed, yet look ye.*

Not true, I say to Alan the Listener. The masochist is a cleverer than we give him credit for. He controls his circumstances and everyone around must dance to his tune. He is far from fear and shame and it's a distance and a half from being under the control of another.

The fly boys who were now in a position of supreme power, unfearing, unashamed, in the confined world of the orange room, would, one day, meet their match. They too would have their trousers round their ankles as a manifestation of inferiority. They would be naked. *We shall not be found naked,* but they would be. That I would like to see. More, I would like to be that power over them. But here, for now, they were the power to be reckoned with and their power over McGraw was not yet complete. They wanted their pleasure to equal their power.

What about some nice music? said a fly boy seated at the table. *Music to go with the sunset. Look at all this shite.* He pointed to the stack of records beside him. *Are these yours?* he asked McGraw. McGraw nodded, and the fly boy pushed them slowly with the barrel of his pistol until the pile slid slowly onto the floor, scattering about our feet.

An unsleeved Schubert impromptu lay coldly at my toes. Number 3 in G-flat on the label around the hole. When I lifted my eyes off the impromptu disc, a fly boy at the table eyed me up through the centre hole in a record that had remained on the table. There in the contact, there in his isolated eye, I foresaw the danger presented to me. It was the danger in his unenlightened eye, the eye that didn't want to see, or to know something important. An eye searching for diversion, damaging distraction. It was just there in front of me, staring me in the eye, the truth about this place, that here in this place was that problem, *all* a problem of distraction. And out of distraction is pain.

I spy with my little eye a batch boy. Or is he a bogie boy? He then flung the record with some force, and with a high degree of accuracy, frisbee-fashion, at McGraw, striking him cleanly with its thin edge on the forehead. McGraw stumbled an inch or so forward held back by the lowered bags, his knees buckling and his buttocks stiffening under a surface layer of fat. Cleg tilted his head back to look down his nose onto his very own stricken pervert. Ah, what enjoyment Cleg exhibited. The pillars of his pleasure were almost entirely in place to support his passion. The circumstances of power, the bodily symptoms, only an action or a word were required to extend him to a full expression of delight. I wanted, in an instant, to destroy that emotional structure by revealing something unknown to Cleg. In an imaginary instant I entertained the idea that McGraw was really Cleg's father. How that would change everything about his enjoyment.

Oedipus and Jocaste, says Alan the Listener, his electric blue eyes now spitting out sparks of new interest.

What experiences were these fly boys capable of having? Of Schubert? Of composition? To what extent were they composed?

In their amplitude what constituted their limits? McGraw having Schubert in his slum house led me to believe something about him that I had not considered before. His own amplitude. Where was it most adequately expressed? When he touched me, maybe he was seeing himself as the pianist touching the piano keys and the sounds I made were the pleasant results of his playing. Sometimes his playing was good and sometimes bad, but when I made no sound at all, then he failed to interpret my silence and I was outside and beyond his power to affect.

What exceptional lads these fly boys were. They were wildly exceptional, but they conformed too. They were here pulling and tugging McGraw and me into their wild ways, unrestrained by common notions and the ways in which they conformed to causes. The essence of their seeing was from their idle street corner existence. From that convergence of streets they could enlarge the single dimension. Knowing these boys and knowing Schubert were different ways of knowing a man, but they both had their wild and exceptional ways.

Schubert was a lively idea for me now. Lively in the sense of stronger to the imagination. I heard the impromptu without hearing a single sound, and was immediately in Schubert's head. The sounds around were banished. Cleg was speaking but he would never speak of Schubert or be in Schubert's mind to hear Schubert speak to him. When I lowered my eyes again the Schubert record had gone from before my feet.

The rhythm of a light and heavy heartbeat, in this rarefied air, of the G flat impromptu paved the way for the courage to be had.

19.

The courageous act—what is it? Where is it? In knowledge? In the unwavering certainty of thought? I thought and how I wavered.

I hadn't uttered a word. I even smiled at the merchants of flyness. To access their friendly fly aspect. I should have opened my mouth and told them about Schubert. To show them that I knew something that they would never in their entire lives understand. From somewhere within me I needed to do something, to say something that pointed to their weakness. But I would never have been able to explain Schubert to them. Schubert in his own relation. The compositional relation.

Courage? Courage not to fear, to be unwavering in wisdom and will in the face of their intimidating actions. Where was that to be found? In my religion? I didn't know how to be courageous in my religion. Just be faithful to it. But is not faith a form of courage?

Courage as something to do with faith or hope seemed weak, not courageous at all, as hope and fear are weak ideas of the mind and courage *had* to be something strong. The church people were essentially weak as hydrated pish. They needed the crowd. All the shouting together to be brave, to feel the fortitude. Faith had to be reassessed in my mind in order to be compatible with courage. But I had no idea how to plant my foot on that path. I had to be strong. Strong in my defence. Certain in my self. My commanding self. My obedient self. The fortress self.

What is faith, what is hope but uncertainty of the mind I kept telling myself? It kept coming back to me in its boundless certainty as that uncertainty. A weakness of wavering thought. I didn't need uncertainty. Courage is a form of love someone said. But how was courage anything at all to do with love? For what indeed is love? Love is as strong as death, says Solomon. I was almost there with him. Burt Lancaster said that love is the morning and the evening star in Elmer Gantry. What was that? Was it the beauty of a thing? Was it the shining certainty? It was the beginning and the end perhaps. Love and beauty coming in full circle

Is genuine hate not a more appropriate companion to courage? Shouldn't we hate more? That was the idea that gripped me as that whole charade continued. Loathing and hate. In an instant I despised the hooded fly boys and McGraw. McGraw slightly less in that instant as he had Schubert in his mind somewhere. Neither had I pity for McGraw being hurt and humiliated in his bare pimpled pathetic arse there before me. That bare arse made me angry, even though it made me laugh too. There was no pity for the arse. Pity involved seeing another as similar to ourselves and seemed to inspire weakness. I denied outright the notion that McGraw and me were alike.

Could hate be useful to courage? Hate arrives at the doorstep of the mind as a pain along with the idea of something that causes it. The pain is a transitive state, an awareness of our movement to a lesser degree of power and perfection, co-extensive with sadness. Ultimately, the disruption of our ability to act. I thought of love. As increase in power, and the ability to act. A unifying principle. How then did I feel powerful with the hatred in me? So, I persisted with the idea that hate and love could be companions in acting courageously. Was this a fiction? Was all this deliberation a fiction?

In the midst of this mess, I took my self off. Who is the bravest person I could think of? Jesus? No, It wasn't even a toss up. 'Twas

Shane. Shane O'Neill? Not a bit of it. Not that mad murdering Irishman. The Earl of backstabbers. No, it was Shane the roving gunman cowboy. The lonesome horseman.

But he's not real, complains Alan the Listener.

Neither real or unreal, I reply. *A man of the pure imagination.*

Make-believe? He pretended not to know. We'd been down this road before.

Nothing of the sort. What example can I send his way to cleanse him of this error? *Starrett's stump. Watch the scene with the tree stump. A troublesome tree stump that clings to homesteader Joe Starrett's earth.*

I know it. It sits right outside his prairie house door. A stump that could have been easily shifted with a team of horses, but Starrett refuses himself that help.

Yes, so what? *Revealing his absolute dedication to the frontier existence in spite of every imminent and immanent threat to life and limb. There is courage. But more, When Shane helps him shift the stump nobility combines with courage.*

Is that all?

Don't you see?

The catechism of masochism, chapter one, prompted Cleg, now back immeasurably close to McGraw. He looked upon the artefact of excitement before and below him with ridicule. What continued to stir McGraw was something of a mystery.

I was still sitting silently. Fortitude was a bastard to get to. Where would I get it in the shite-scented orange-illuminated hole where evil is no distance at all and cowardice an easier option?

This was not a place for women after all. There would be no women. No sweet smells and softness. No plump red lips and long fingers. The man McGraw was in suitable disgrace, gracelessly bowing and silent now of promises. I still wanted his promises to be true. His head was angled forward, his chin resting on his chest, like a naked madman drained of desire. And this was his Victorian asylum. All longing and wanting in retreat.

His eyes sunk low in his sockets, like moons slipping out of orbit, either a pleasurable response to near ecstasy or just exhaustion. He seemed to be in a trance. If ecstasy, it would have been a ceremony only open to him, a private performance. Cleg seemed to be annoyed that he was excluded from McGraw's orbit, by the apparent absence of his pervert, and was soon questioning whether McGraw's perceptible excitement derived from any form of presently operating desire.

Detecting a real rise in tension, I felt like removing myself—like McGraw—once more to the real world of Schubert. The G flat (the vinyl artefact that is) crackled on. It skipped and stuck in the grooves, , but, insofar as the piece of music was nothing of the audible, I could find myself totally with the idea of the impromptu itself, far away from the increasing insanity. The artefact in fact, frustratingly misunderstood by Cleg and the fly boys as simple sound, as interrupted and repeated noise of notes, erected more and more, swifter and swifter, an atmosphere of lunacy and menace. The gentle succession of notes of the andante, where the record needle seemed to stick most, seemed to disturb any restraint. It soon became a necessary accompaniment to their particular lack of composure, so the record played on.

Tell me your secret, whispered Cleg into McGraw's ear. *What's the secret of that big boner? Don't you wish for a woman to share this with? Or don't you get your root with women?* Cleg's right foot stamped forcefully on the floor with a regular beat and for no obvious motive. It kept me from absenting myself from the circumstances. *What is your nature, McGraw? We all have a nature. What makes us us. What makes you you? What is your shame? What do you conceal?* Now these words were said in time with the stamping foot. From the wall

Cleg lifted the picture and presented it to McGraw's glassy gaze. *We don't have to ask who that is, because we're in the know.* This was all getting so despairing and tiresome. The tone in which it was said was despairing. An expert needling whine claiming dubious knowledge. What it said and the direction in which it was moving was despairing. But what was this now?

How could you be so cruel to that wee girl? How did you get away with it? How? How did you do it? How? Smack! An open Cleg hand came down hilariously onto the back of McGraw's greasy bop. Made me lurch forward from my tense seated pose, to a rigid forward angle with my chest almost resting on my knees. Cleg rubbed his hand that hit on his trousers to remove the McGraw grease. *I think we'll have to make you pay for what you've done to that wee girl, seeing the fucking Brit Ulster law didn't see fit to apply some justice.* It was three thirty-three a.m. when I glanced at my watch with as much subtly as I could.

20.

The truth shall make you free. But, *suppose truth to be a woman,* asks Nietzsche. There was a woman. Or a girl. A truthful soul. Her truth was not in propositions, it was in her acts. In her body was a model for truth. We found one another in church and walked and talked together after the Sunday service. We became close. She was perfect. We were perfectly close. At peace together, the sort of peace that passeth all understanding. It thus had the mark of God stamped upon it. We were believers who believed in God and ourselves. She was kind and she was fun. Her lips didn't lie when I kissed them. I lay awake in bed with her name on my lying lips, repeating it.

What was her name? asks the Listener. *You have not uttered her name.*

And it will remain unsaid. It's sacred.

I think I know it anyway.

Well… we had the peace that passeth all understanding.

Yes yes.

That is why understanding can ruin everything. Or a form of it. You want a certain certainty. It is called *an understanding*. That is what I wanted.

But you had a certain understanding. What certain certain understanding did you want?

Yes, we had a certain understanding, you are right. What made it certain was holding her cold hands, having those cold hands on my warm

brow, having no space between our bodies when we walked, her smile
at my smile, all that. But the certainty I wanted was the certainty of
words, unlike Shane and Starrett over the tree stump where everything
was made clear in silence. That stated certainty. Like a contract. She
soon saw that.

Before the desire for words there was her body which seemed
to be more and more than you'd think a body could ever be. Like
Nietzshe said, *The truly surprising thing is the body.* She was small,
superbly trim, and dark with a sublime smile always and forever
in her eyes. She walked both with the grace of God and freely
with grace itself. Never did she take a step that was clumsy. The
clothes she wore, the delicate flowing silks and satins, wore me
down to my bare passion. Her dress was emotional language, its
lightness never failed to express a unique body of emotional truth.
It possessed me like the spirit didn't.

The route of the after service walks themselves got longer, the
general pace of walking got slower—the talking got deeper—the
direction less defined, except perhaps for the direction we each set
in our minds. And the longer we dallied in our danders the further
we burrowed into each other's affections.

The pain of every parting led me to a confounding sadness,
bound entirely by her and confined entirely to her. From the very
first moment of her absence I had her name on my lips and the
damned duration of separation inclined to eternity. But, I was
never sure that she had my name on hers. And as that thought
became more and more prominent I embarked upon a mission
to find a form of words that she could assent to in order that all
was clear between us. It would take my mind out of commotion
and lay it to rest. It took me months to settle on a formula. When
I did, I rehearsed it like a holy creed. It was on one of the very
first autumn after Sunday service walks, on a swiftly cooling and
darkening evening, that I readied my words. But she spoke first.

You are so cruel to me, she said. I laughed, but she insisted. *Why are you so cruel to me?* Her eyes kept smiling long after the words had gone. Her head tilted to one side inviting a response. We walked a bit further, slowly in silence. The space that appeared between us was never there before, as if we now needed it to think clearly, and when it was time to go our own ways I looked at her again for an answer. *Tell me what you mean?* She just continued to smile. I said that I would be grateful for an answer in words and not in a smile, as she had told me in words. She said it was in words, that the words were right there in the smile. *The key is in the smile*, she said, *in fact it is all here.* With outstretched arms she demonstrated her body. I said it was cruel to be so enigmatic. She said the smile was what it was.

The Shane smile. The smile to Starrett that consumed all doubt and suspicion. Sealed a unity. *The key is in the smile.* I considered the smile. I asked her to give it to me again, but there was nothing given quite like the original. I lived with it night and day. That bloody smile! Was it a truthful smile? Was it the very same smile every time I thought of it and every time it greeted me? The same, the same, what makes something the same? The smile was and it was not. In a rare moment of clarity I thought it might mean that my restraint was unnecessary. It was *cruel* to keep her waiting, to keep her walking on that meandering, directionless path that I thought so pleasant in itself. That bloody smile! *The smile is what it is,* she endlessly repeated. *Well, I am lost, lost… lost to know,* I said.

Almost at a loss, ready to forfeit the matter, without another thing to say, I thought the very thing I did not want to think. My own body, lying open before her to see, revealing what I could not see myself. Was my cruelty really in an unconscious lust? In my hands when I touched her. In my lips. She saw it in my body. And every time she looked upon my body she saw something that she didn't want to see. A clear idea of a desire. In her smile was a judgement, the body and the idea in one. How would *I* know?

Then something else came to me out of that poisonous place of confused recollection, the huckster store of duplicated notions strung out on the conscious mind. I did something cruel once. But not entirely heartless. I felt a maverick urge. It wasn't in my nature. It opened a fault in it. I remembered. In the yard. He came to me smiling his loyal smile.and immediately on seeing it I began to act like a madman. It was a madness to express mastery over him. He was beaten and then comforted. I denied that it opened up some fissure out of which spilled disturbing desires, but denial or no denial, I began to explore the universal world of ideas of the smooth, the soft, the tight and the being of such things on the body. Did she know this? She knew something. Just like Cleg knew something about McGraw.

21.

String them together, said a fly boy out of his dark corner. *Strip them and string the fucking homos together. Tight. Face to face.* It was a voice I knew. That sad authorship. *That's what they came for, to be together, isn't it?*

Nothing outside now had any bearing on what was inside McGraw's house. My neck stiffened and cramped. I dropped my head forward and stared at the filthy floor. So there we all were as extended filth. The filthy Celtic fellows. There we were, McGraw and me, the filthy odd men out. There it was. The filthy circumstance. *As you were,* says the army command. And we were as we were. Slipping in as we were, and not entirely as instances of emptiness.

Shane asked for the gun to be put down. *I'd like it to be my idea, he* said when ordered off Starrett's land at gunpoint. Nothing here would or could be my idea. What Stoic courage could I resurrect here and now? Strange that I might have thought of this first instead of the source of salvation. Why? Because I thought of Shane.

The lamb's book of life, I muttered. Do these boys know it? I thought of the God fearing homesteaders. That God fearing was really simple stoicism. Faith in themselves. But the final judgement has nothing of the stoic in it.

The filth on the floor. More and more. My lazy gaze spent an incalculable moment tracing a path along the floor to the open door and to intense darkness. Cleg before us with the picture in his hand becoming impatient. Making sure McGraw still had it in his mind, he jabbed the picture in his face, which was a picture of distress and despair. Cruelty was coming my way. Heartless cruelty. But what comfort would follow? What future? Schubert was still crackling away. I listened. I listened more. I heard the most extraordinary thing. My body. Not the Cartesian object, not the contingent cause of ideas, not the inferior body, just the body. The thinking body.

McGraw was now on his bony knees, forced down there by Cleg, the individual bones heard grinding on the cold, hard floor. His bare knees impregnated with dirt. He could barely hold that position. Perfectly expressing his pain was his mouth, opened to an unnatural width, stretching his moist lips to an almost impossible tightness. The silent scream. Not a sound exited that chamber. Cleg, his torturer, was above him, spluttering with laughter, inspired by the incredulity at what was prodigious in the McGraw sexual stamina.

String them both together, insisted once again that sad, shadowy author in the corner.

You can only get a hard on if you are enjoying something, right? Isn't that right enough though? Cleg spun around on his heels looking for his audience. *I mean, from personal experience I know. When I am pointing a gun at some cunt's head and about to pull the trigger, empty a chamber, guess what? I get a good boner. Like when I split that Protestant fucker's head open with an axe. That tells me I am enjoying it, so it must be right. And some bloke told me that some cunts who are about to die get a boner. What do they know on their death beds?*

Listening to the body, I seemed unable to think at all in a straight line, or at the required speed relative to Cleg's swiftly composed words. I accelerated off at different angles to other destinations. To elsewhere. And then slowed until I was at rest in pursuit of judgements, affirmations and denials.

I mean, you wouldn't get a hard-on if you were watching your granny dying, now would you? But what if you did? And what about if she was dying and some arse tried to fuck her? Then you might get a hard-on laughing at it.

The G flat slowed, no longer music, it entered the thinking body as a compositional rhythm. It was a space through which my thought accelerated to the place of my own granny's swiftly rotting body. I saw her decelerating in her death bed. Decomposing at speed. Blinking slow, speech slow. Nothing else moved. Her eyes surrounded by dark circles, disease circling, a circle of waiters around her bed. We came as we were to see her end. And then the sudden unexplained rushing around when something was happening after long hours of sitting and waiting for something to happen. Death. The lifeless big woman inspiring excessive life and movement all around.

Knelt beside the naked McGraw, my naked body told me something. With pressure on my shoulders I had been forced downward by Cleg's strong hands just as McGraw had been. My knees bent slowly, with resistance. The pressure increased slightly. I resisted slightly. How far should I go? Just until the pressure stopped. It was the same pressure applied to your head by Bilko the winking barber and the same resistance.

There on my knees my body revealed that it was ready. Ready to be formed anew. Ready to receive and be affected. I detected a total absence of holiness. Nothing of Shradrach, Meshach, and Abed-nego in the fiery furnace. No praying. No conversation with God. No spirit to come and stand at my side, or four-squarely like the pastor. I was firmly rooted to this place, to this space, predestined in a modular manner to be so. This unholy kneeling was all part of the plan, that was no plan, but I was foreseen to kneel here, I was foreseen as forsaken. Forsaken here now in front of McGraw. In what way will I be affected? How great will it be? My capacities here were unknown as were my needs. My own mysterious amplitude.

A wild gust of air struck my smooth skin. A massive wind that blew up the black hallway from the front door. Not the mighty rushing wind. Not the wind that bloweth, as whispered by the preacher. A cry in the wilderness beyond.

That's the spirit departing, said Cleg, and ordered someone to go into the black hallway to shut the front door.

A certain amount of rope was found. In the city of rope. Money for old rope the old folk would say but no money changed hands here. Several strips were in the hands of Cleg and the sad author who had shifted his arse and shuffled from the shadowy corner that he'd made his own.

Who's going to be the hangman? said Cleg. They were establishing a rhythm. One that me and McGraw were encouraged to take up.

What are you boys good at? continued Cleg. *We, us here, are good at some things. So we are told. Not in so many words. Sometimes words of tribute are not possible.*

We know what they are good at, said the sad author out of his shadow.

What would establish McGraw and me adequately for Cleg and his men in this given encounter? When our bodies were openly defined to them by our desires, revealed initially as instances of unrestrained obedience to their desires, and transformed into willing participants of a newly constituted set of relations that included them. In that, a form of identity between us and them was being forged.

So, when McGraw and me were nakedly upright and face to face, body tight to body, roped together by the neck, our balls ringed with rope and tethered one set to the other, groin given to groin, we kissed when we were told to kiss, exchanged saliva when were told to, entwined tongues when we told to, thrust erect cock upon erect cock when we were told to, until it appeared that we were total lovers for them, acting spontaneously, with our own inner effort. And we did. In this very unique place, our clumsy, discrete responses to orders, dissolved into one unanalysable total act, that included Cleg and the fly boys, their ridicule, their provocation, their commands, their repeated interruptions to prolong the performance and provoked desperation in delay, the whole ritual that enslaved us to them, was no longer set apart, but constituted a bond between us. It fell just short of a worded contract. No everlasting arms to lean on here.

Soon enough I found myself untied and in praying posture, my elbows rested lightly on the lumpy settee cushions. The posture was familiar, as at my bedside every single night before bed and before God. The same posture here but no desire to call on the saviour to rescue me from my ungodly circumstance. The numinous next to nothing. Abandoned by the inescapable, immanent God, a new vocabulary of immanence was forcefully established.

Ultimately the language would be formal, with detailed set rituals, strict rules of encounter, extravagant demonstrative, suspenseful drama, names altered according to status. A composition of relations pre-established.

With McGraw at my back, breathing the devil's hot breath on my neck, lifting me off my knees and driving into my arse, the inflexible fantasy that will stand for all time, remained here merely in fledgling form. I had my name change however,

McGraw whispering *little Pauline* in my ear. Oh God! *Eli, Eli, lama sabachthani!*

Cleg interrupted the vigorous poetic rhythm to issue in a private whisper something of a confession to me. *I'm jerking this pervert about and he knows why.* The picture of the girl was lying on the settee. *But that is what we do, that is what we're going to be doing all the time. We've been jerked about for years, so now it's our turn. We have the means now.* He produced his gun from his belt and kissed the barrel. *A lot of people are going to be fucked about before this is finished, I promise you.* That was Brian Donleavy in *Beau Geste.* As Sergeant Markoff always promising punishment. I listened from under the man McGraw's body, my head turned to the side on the settee to pay attention to what Cleg had to say. The weight was suffocating, like McGraw's experience under his dying da. McGraw was soon finished with me and pulled himself away.

My moist eyes closed tightly so that I could live in blind darkness for as long as I could, for in that darkness there was the possibility of sleep, a discreet little sleep, with pleasant notions to pass the time. But before any such desired ideas appeared on the dark canvas there was a cold stroke on my cheek that roused me.

Eyes open now, I saw at my side McGraw kneeling as I was. A preposterous pair. His glasses lay before him broken on the settee. And passing in front of me was a waving gun issuing a command, requiring me to stand and take a position behind McGraw's bare and trembling fat arse. An more amusing sight indeed. The exposure, the quaking fat. The head facing forward, bobbing up and down, rotating left and right, but unable to view its own state of stupidity. The anti-divine comedy was here. Anti-Devine. Thinking McGraw like Andy Devine was comical. How could the hosts in heaven fail to laugh at this? Cleg's attention landed on me like the big Cleg fly on a fresh lump of shite. The enjoyment was all over his face.

Even it up. Get even. An arse for an arse, he insisted, with an increased enthusiasm in my direction. *Like for like. He fucked you now you can get even. Don't let people fuck you and let the chance to get even slip away. That is life. That is courage. Getting even. You don't want to be a cowardly shite, do you? An empty skite. Even-steven, get the fuck even. Fuck that foul bastard even. Fuck him to evenness. Fuck him fair.* Cleg was almost entering the world of the poet and preacher. Not far from poetry to prayer. But he wasn't a poet. Nor a prayer. He was a fucker. His voice rhythm was like a regular fuck. He fucked people up. Fucked their brains out. The others sat in silence and watched him. Silence was their speciality. Had they nothing to say? Silence swept in from the hallway too. From the watchman who had not returned after shutting the front door.

The cold gun barrel continued to point the way for my warm and willing cock. To McGraw's waiting arse. Cleg repeated his words of ritual retribution. I placed myself behind McGraw, held him tightly around the waist, welcomed the warmth and made a few incompetent thrusts. But nothing came of it, except a moment of clarity in a confused joy, a realisation, a real power of mind affirming its own body, that took into account the precise circumstance. A place occupied by law abidance, where I didn't pray. I could almost see that the man with the gun, Cleg, would *have* to have the gun, would agree even to have the gun. I would make it a requirement. Together with the frustration suffered by McGraw.

The sound of Schubert was suddenly completely absent. A new composition was emerging. Cleg sat beside McGraw with the gun pressed hard to his temple, mixing fear with the frustration. I could see the temple being violated. The tip of the gun barrel prodding the pressure point. I stood up and back and watched and wiped my brow of something wet. I delighted in a bare body that had contracted with the intense cold, and hunger, leaving it almost without definition. I placed my hands on my bare, bony hips and found the pose exciting.

McGraw was prompted to stand, Cleg's gun still painfully prodding his temple. *What is it you like about young Seamus here? Those lips? His lovely long black wavy hair? His feminine hips?* He pointed at each as he mentioned them. *Look how he stands. He stands for you. Do you have a name for him... or her? Oh I know.* I liked the idea of standing for something, taking a stand. Then Cleg stared at McGraw as never before. *Is there love in this slimy horn of yours McGraw? You have some fucking staying power. But it's not love. God only knows what it is.*

Then there was a moment when seemingly nothing happened. But it was significant. It was that pause. Not a word. It was like the end process of youthful play, when boredom and exhaustion takes over and friends just sit silently and happily in each other's presence. Now seemed to be *the moment of decision.* That's how the Pastor Davy Prebble referred to the crucial, critical time period for sinners to repent. It was a critical moment. For the word. What word next?

Alas, the word wasn't with us. We waited for the words to come. The word in fly boy flesh. The word that might make us powerful, the word that might make us cruel. The word that might make us laugh. The mighty word of wit. Cruel wit. Contemptuous wit. Rude wit. Dirty wordy wit. We were told not to say dirty words. The mother was the guardian of words. She would skelp our legs into lumps with a bamboo stick, if she heard us saying something dirty. We were reminded of the stain of sin, the black spot, yet, in that time of special productivity, on her knee, she taught us the dirty rhyme with the *fart* word in it. *There was a wee woman of ninety-two, she blew a wee fart and away it flew, over the mountains and down the lane and into the Farmer's window pane. The farmer came out with a rusty gun, shot the wee fart and away in run, over the mountains and down the wee lane and back into the wee woman's bum again.* Then we laughed because she laughed. She was in control. She controlled the mood. I shouted out Torrest Fucker once instead of Forrest Tucker, and I feared for a moment, but she was in a good mood.*warm*

22.

The reality of perfect imperfection. When I kept my eyes peeled I saw perfect necessity where you might expect to find only contingency. The fly boys in the orange glare seemed to announce themselves to the beat of the big drum of contingency as madly as the Orangeman beats the big Lambeg drum for King Billy on the twelfth. It was like the defining *shout* demanded by another source to shut you up.

A form, an essence of sorts, something that assigned a degree of stability would appear before you, yet it could also be appreciated as a composition of the accidental. In the absence of a strong, governing influence they were wild and wayward, unpredictable, uncertain of motivation, and yet that is precisely what made them the perfect raw material of the slave and submissive, easily educated in hatred, vengeance and cruelty. This was the essence of their imperfection. A lack of power even though they felt power. The desperate desire to be an inferior, a mere function of a superior will, expressed perfectly in a consciousness which emerged specifically to reflect the immediate external higher authority and ultimately the eternal nature of things.

Their immediate subordination was to Cleg. Whatever they said, Cleg said first, whatever they performed, were actions obedient to Cleg. The greater authority was *the cause*, but the fly boys only knew it through the glass darkly that was Cleg's mind. *Self-determination for us and our people*, was their unconvincing cry, but they had no idea what self-determination was

I was thinking of these fly boys in the same way as I thought of old Shubert, condemned through slowness and little latitude for independent action. The backward person was well described, so slow there was no progress.

So what of necessity? I saw it in a flash, the hierarchy of things distributed appropriately. Particularly in this arrangement before me but also, though in a weaker intuition, the wider arrangement of things. Things now and things to come.

I asked myself, were these boys beyond the grasp of goodness, the good will. I had no answer as I lacked an adequate idea of goodness myself. So, I examined my own actions and asked myself if they were good or bad. Neither had I any idea how to answer that question. I knew what Spinoza said: *We neither strive for, nor will, neither want nor desire anything because we judge it to be good: we judge something to be good because we strive for it, will it, want it, desire for it,* but those words led me to consider desire and not goodness. Desire in that moment, standing with Cleg and the humiliated McGraw was born as a particular effort, not merely as a consciousness of appetite, but a consciousness that it was mine. The lack of hate now reflected a movement towards a reason that manifested a form of pleasure and confidence.

23.

Alan is fast becoming more than a listener. His tribute to the English architect in verse has a compositional affect on our relationship. I am not a mere function of him, nor is he of me, neither ego opposing the other, or considered external to the other. In the insubordinate unconscious we speak as one.

The English Architect on a Sticky Wicket

Drawing, drawn, drawn out
Led from a cosy lofty space
His official place
By far below bellows

Young Celtic fellows
In their sporting devotion
The source of a commotion
Precise lines blurring.

Designs he has
This placid stranger
On the construct of peace
Twixt work and play

'Tween fellows and he
The plan, the view
To purchase a crease
In pastures green

This old Angle so benign
The peace he finds
Applying soothing voice balm
To claim the Celtic calm

That accord achieved
In that elevated peace withdrawn
Plans he weaves
For plots not his own

On other drawing board
A deadly plan is hatching
From a single chamber
A designer death despatching

And, up in his airy room
The fixer fails to see
His life looms nearer inevitably
To his pretty emerald tomb

In pastures green
At his crease unaware
Young Celtic fellows declare
A joy by English Architect unseen.

Distraction. Those boys of badness. The cowardly crew of
rebels. Weepy wet little cunts if you had them on their own. It just

was not cricket. Those fools. The tools of fooldom not following the rules of bat and ball.

He asked us if we played cricket. The five or six of us playing in the entry. He, the erect English architect, who came down to us from his place of peace on high. One summer dusk he drew a last line for the day. He put down his pencil on his drawing board. He raised himself, descended his many stairs and came out into the open, moseying towards us with a dragged, weighty step. We judged it to be a handicap, halted all our noisy business. A heavy ball that was repeatedly blasted against a large, corrugated iron gate of the cement factory. We rallied ourselves and waited. He came, came slowly and stopped, holding himself at a safe distance from us in our firmly held ground. The concrete entry where we often had to take a stand. It was disputed land, between those who wanted it empty and free of noise, infidels to entertainment, hostile to laughter and fun. From their upstairs portals, from inside their coward's castles, they declared their dissatisfaction with our joyful racket, shouting their absurd threats, wanting only their own mad, miserable din, of TV and domestic argument, in their ears. No peelers ever came to clear us off. So the ground held was the ground that ground them down, their remote, withdrawn declarations being nothing to fear. Laughing in their bloated, frustrated faces and endowing them with nicknames was a pleasant pastime.

His English was foreign. This architect English. We followed the line of his pointing finger and were guided in our thinking by long lines of words in a low volume, rigid, breathless monotone, abruptly intersected with long intakes of air. *Take a vertical from the base of that garage. Up, straight up to the long glass dormer. That's my vantage point, from where I watch you all play. And your play is a wonderful thing to watch.* In spite of the foreign nature of the words and the way with words, we thought we had the measure of him. A parallel measure however, he on his train of thought and we on ours.

After a longer pause, that was not merely to suck in air, but to broach the real purpose for his appearance before us, he continued less confidently. *Yes, a wonderful thing to behold, but not to hear. Up there in my workplace I need a measure of silence.* Then we were all on the same track. A track we were invited to take to see his workplace and look down upon our playplace.

We followed him up his many stairs until we were ushered into a place of startling order and uniformity. A distance and a half away from our chaotic homes. The order was reinforced by cleanliness. No dust, no dirty or peeling paint work, no cracked plaster. A smoothness unknown. Nor the fusty smell of damp. No lazily discarded objects. No piles of junk. Just overwhelming and intimidating order, in dimmed and atmospheric light.

I go to work here, he said. Going to work at home was a contradiction to me. Work took you away from home, and you had to create a mood of strength to overcome the withdrawal. I feared it just as I feared my first day at school.

The English architect corralled us and guided us toward a glass dormer window that ran from ceiling to floor, jutting out in a geometrical form, more or less half octagonal, well beyond the walls. From there we were invited to look upon the place of play absent of play and noise, and consider the absence of our own presence. He had taken us from it and exhibited it to us as he required it. The place where our best moments were had and best memories made and future joy expected. It was viewed in silence.

Back in the centre of the room we stood as a tightly knit group around the architect's drawing board while he explained the significance of the intersecting, parallel and converging, lines, the geometrical shapes, and his precise relationship to them. *I am no artist he said, the shapes are all important. As is the plan. The work here is unfinished here.* He drew our attention to photographs pinned to the top of the board, of bombed Belfast buildings that had to be rebuilt. *I design the new buildings to replace these shells. To keep the place from going to the devil. It is very exacting work. And dangerous.* He was English and an architect and that, we soon realised, was indeed a dangerous identity to possess.

Then, as interest waned in his abstract world of lines and shapes, came the cricket question. Yes, we told him, we played it in the entry like everything else. There were stumps painted on the outside wall of the cement factory. But we told him it was probably not cricket the way he knew it. It was a perilous Irish game that we played.

Cricket can be dangerous, he said, *it is the skill of the cricketer that makes it less so. His discipline.* We knew that. A ball of concentrated cork fired by one man at another at ninety miles per hour can be dangerous. We showed the architect our cricketing injuries. My brother Frankie pointed to the permanent bump on the bridge of his nose, and Kieron pulled his jaws apart to incredible and alarming dimensions to display a cleanly broken central incisor. Trouser legs and shirt sleeves were enthusiastically rolled up to reveal less permanent injuries. We explained that we played the gentlemanly game, not with the normal cricket ball, which was not always available, but with a golf ball, often late into the evenings in semi-darkness, with only the weak illumination of a solitary gas lamp on the wall above the batsman and his painted wall wickets to assist the senses and the quality of judgement.

Almost instantaneously the acute architect brain had seized upon the horror of such a game. He shook his head with mother country disapproval, the look in his eyes condemning us for our mad maladministration of the genteel and cultured game. In fact he probably didn't even see the whole picture. The Irish adaptation was aimed to increase the excitement and the moments of humour, but ultimately neither of these had an importance greater than the simple undertaking of being brave enough to be part of it. To take a stand there as a lonely batsman, to be the helpless fielder, with a golf ball ricocheting out of and through the darkness was considered daring indeed.

But, what was all this to an English architect? *Do you see these plans here,* he said, pointing to his drawing board. *Well, I have another plan, one that will make everyone happy. One that will allow us all to get on together.* He moved to a deep cupboard on the other side of the room, opened it and pulled out a long and weighty bag. He dragged it over to his drawing board and to our feet.

Out of it he produced a cricket set of faultless quality and completeness. Everything was there; bats, stumps, bails, leg pads, protective gloves, brand new, deep red cork balls. Not a toy, the real thing to be played in earnest. It had the smell of something not to be touched, like the antique furniture in Kaismann's antique shop on the Dublin Road. Or the artefacts in the Ulster Museum, where we occasionally went for a sobering experience of untouchable beauty and a good laugh at the daft looking mummies.

The architect took the bat of beautifully grained, yellowing willow in his hands. He rubbed the tips of his fingers down the smooth, flat surface. Beautiful, almost no resistance there. Tranquillising to watch. We were each given a moment to place our fingers on the bat to do the same.

Take yourselves away from the hard, grey ground. Find some soft area of green and use it. And it's all yours. Then out of the bag, from some integral pocket, he pulled a small bottle.

Linseed oil, he announced. *Extract of flax. Mercilessly squeezed from the seeds. A preservative. A life giver. A protector.* It was held up and looked at with a special reverence. He unscrewed the top and poured a drop of the thick amber liquid out on to the tip of his forefinger which was held up before for us to see. He then demonstrated its use. With a soft, virgin cloth he rubbed the oil into the wood in such a way that made the whole task seem very personal, very intimate. He studied our faces as he performed the routine. We each eagerly performed the task in turn. *It'll last a lifetime if you treat it well,* he said, his voice almost as smooth as the oil he rubbed into the bat. It was a comment designed to draw us in closer, to hook us, and, before we knew it, to have us assent to the deal.

What proceeded from this? If we accepted it, were we obliged to take ourselves out of our concrete haven to pastures green as honorary English boys to play the English game the way it should be played?

Our natural disposition was to mock the English as sissies. English men pushed prams for their wives. The wives here wouldn't ask that of their men, for gentlemanliness to that degree was effeminacy. On that Irish Protestants and Catholics were agreed.

We were also keen to persist with our version of their game with the golf ball as it was a form of mockery. It mocked the English gentility and tried to affirm Celtic hardness, fearlessness and courage without ever considering the elements of stupidity attached to it. And we were indeed a stupid race in many of our efforts.

In the end we had to pass judgement on the English architect. Was he a courageous soul who came out to us where we stood fearless when no one else would, the ones that shouted down upon us from their high windows? Or was he like the civilised man offering trinkets to the daft savages. We realised it was not a case of either/or. He was a courageous, civilised man thinking he was dealing with savages.

So, we bestowed upon the Englishman a limited respect. This restricted approval meant however, that whilst we accepted his cricket set, took ourselves to the distant greenery of the park and rubbed the thick oil into the wood of bat and stumps, we did so out of a restricted sense of duty. Soon visits to the green spaces became less and less of an occurrence and the amber oil hardened and dried as discipline for the task waned. Cricket resumed in the entry and the equipment was adapted to its new concrete surroundings. The bat soon cracked up the middle. The rest of the equipment was mislaid in somebody's house and lost forever.

Back in our natural place, we often looked up to the architect's window to our world and wondered what he thought of us. Continuing to reflect upon the nature of the whole episode, we began to give him a less restricted form of respect. Nothing of the sort from the brutes who came to him in the night, knowing him only as an English architect, sneaked up his many stairs, and bowled him out of existence forever in his neat and ordered place of work.

24.

The pose I adopted in front of McGraw and Cleg and the inattentive fly boys was an act that was not an act. That is to say it was not a deception. It was not a deceiving spirit that inspired it. But what it inspired was a form of sleep, an abandonment of all that was present. I may have slipped into a memory mode, a memory system, a process that removes you from immediate events that have an information value only, and from the conditions which determine that value. Sleep, but not any sleep, a determined sleep that wakened the soul. Let me ask this: Is there a thinking that is not such and such an idea? It is an act, an interaction. An unconscious proposition in action. Never mind that, the pose was not a sufficient act in itself, even if it was the decisive moment in taking a stand. What further requirement was necessary? To select what corresponds to this haughty pose. Then determine what powers I had in this alignment.

The father would sing his favourite song that was not a hymn but was hymn-like: *Pale hands, where are you now?* McGraw where is your pale backside now? I stretched a foreign black satin glove over my own thin pale hand until it reached my elbow and placed the gloved hand back on my naked hip. What a sense of the solitary. An emergence of the individual. *If you are never solitary, you are never religious.* Here I was in Beulah land. God had left me as a companion to be replaced by my own company. There was a distinct feeling that this was neither the beginning nor the end of something but the middle. A sense of maturity in this middle. Swept up in a flash into a collective enthusiasm. To an expression of the ritual and rule which were already known.

Where had I found the glove? On the small table with the metal legs. Left there draped over a gun. Now there was movement that belonged. Someone fully appreciated the circumstance, the pose that was the taking of a stand, the stopping of a retreat.

I lifted the picture from the settee with the gloved hand and looked closely at the portrait of the young woman who seemed to cause so much concern. At the same time the general circumstances became apparent. Deserted. Silent. In the orange light. I still had Schubert in my head and Cleg's last whispered words. He had taken me into his confidence before he disappeared. He requested something. I had asked him if Malachy Sloane was one of his fly boys. He lifted his mask over his mouth and smiled. *Malachy, Malachy, Malachy. Buster Keaton we call him. A humourless hallion. He misunderstands everything, and has to be put right. If he is, he is alright. He has found his horizons here with us. He warned us of you and McGraw. You two look like one sorry sick individual. With McGraw you're aligning yourself with a very sick small world. As small as it can be. Jesus that slimy fucker. Look at you when we saw you. A slouching cocksucker. I know how these creeps work. They'll keep you for their very own until you're no good to man or beast. But just one act now and your horizons will expand all over the place. I'm a sly fucker I know.* He *is* a fly sly fucker, I thought. I could be his cunt and his mucker though. Where is McGraw?

I went in search of McGraw with the gun in the gloved hand. It felt so fine, either allowing the weight of the weapon to pull my hand down fully to my side or lifting it with my lean arm to a firing position. McGraw was somewhere basking like a white whale in his own solitude. What land was he in? Not my Beulah land. Nakedly, to the exclusion of all else I sought him out. What time was it? The time was up for McGraw, Cleg's fictitious figure. He was before me and before me. And when he was before me I anticipated his demise. He was the obstacle to the formation of a free flowing fantasy. I quietly sung my little song. *Have you heard the story of sticky McGraw? He bored a hole in the wall and that's all.*

I had taken careful steps out of the orange room into the dark hall, elegantly on tiptoes as if in the confines of stilettos. Resting attention on that particular discomfort, I composed the most outrageous imaginings, broken after an unknown period of time, by the realisation that in my spare hand I held, with a high degree of delicacy, McGraw's precious picture. Out of a momentary consideration of the picture, the gift that was McGraw's monologies of his school days, surfaced. His confinement to misery from birth, humbled at every turn. Old Peabody the science teacher mastered him. I laughed inside at McGraw's detailed descriptions of his every humiliation. The beatings, the incarcerations, the imaginative public exhibitions of his most sensitive insecurities.

A shadow appeared before me in the hall together with a powerful odour of a soaking wet day in a busy pawnshop. Then the flat blackness vanished, leaving only the smell and a cold draught from the open front door. In this given instant, this unseparated instance, this intentional stance, in this restricted infinity, I wavered between that door and another. One exit, one entrance. But which was which? I listened to the pressing silence, to the body and felt again the weight of the gun in my gloved hand, which was the precise moment I felt the weight of freedom in necessity.

I found the Irish McGraw in his unwelcoming parlour at the front of the house, the room adjacent to the orange room. Only a short distance on my tiptoes. *There is no courage as great as that born of utter desperation*, but was this act before me courageous? What was the *in-spite-of* aspect to it? I was not desperate in the general sense, but a form of desperation visited me powerfully in the present restricted circumstance, manifest in a degree of unrest.

When I stepped into the room it was, briefly, a time without activity, no time, and a space with nothing situated, no space. That was the effect of a discerning passage of accelerated thought. A musical interlude, a premonition of death. My immediate concern now, when this brief hiatus ended, was to lay the lying man McGraw to rest relative to my unrest.

Cleg's pervert was on a couch, naked on his back, with his head turned to the side. His legs were bound together at the ankles with the same rope that had bound us both together earlier. His arms disappeared behind his back so I assumed they were also bound. I leaned over him and, in the difficult light, detected no significant movement. Placing the gun barrel on to his temple and closing in on him, I sung, *Over the bridge there'll be no sorrow, over the bridge there'll be no pain*, until I felt his breath on my skin, saw his eyelids flicker and his silver nose hairs vibrate.

His head swung around slowly. His eyelids edged apart. I inched my own head away to an appropriate distance—that allowed the gun to remain on his skull—and placed the picture flat over my face. Giving him a second or two to divine what was before him, room enough for a half smile was my impression, I reflected upon this presentation *sub specie aeternitatis* whilst easing the trigger back with my satin finger. Here, at this informal juncture, was an agreeably arranged chamber piece. A natural order of bodies in opposition, maximum and minimum in their respective thresholds, in advance and retreat, transformed both in their peculiarities, one increasing in powerful distribution, assigning an appropriate end to the other. A time of kindling was nigh. The becoming-to-be of death of the freely evil, earthy McGraw and the burning birth of me. Truth, the eternal voice in time, having no truce with the lie, had spoken. Nothing more to be said.

Acknowledgments

Special thanks to my agent Pamela Malpas for her friendship, patience, perseverence and endless endeavour in the business of acting on my behalf.

Immense gratitude to Dan Wickett, Matt Bell & Steve Gillis at Dzanc for their significant contribution to the development and final production of this book.

I am indebted once again to Eileen O'Neill, who, through photographic detective work and an incredible mnemic capacity, re-engaged me with Belfast memories that long separation had almost erased. Her steadfast friendship and support have been significant.